A Reconciliation With Death

by Cody George

"This is a brilliant angle... in apocalyptic fiction to give a story a refreshing feel... This book was a great look at the intimate lives of apocalyptic survivors." - **Writing Werewolf**

"Rather than being an action-packed disaster tale, *A Reconciliation with Death* is a slower, more meditative web of stories – one which asks pertinent questions about the ways in which we deal with trauma, with change, and with global and personal apocalypses.

It does this by following a number of characters through the epidemic and its aftermath. We meet Joey, an orphaned boy, and the therapist who works with him. We encounter bizarre communes and conspiracy theorists, panicking people and grieving people, all of whom are trying to retain or return to something like normality as the world falls apart around them.

These characters are extraordinarily well-realised." - **Neon Books**

"...the different voices are striking in how unique they sound and how real they feel; George really knows how to put us in a character's head... While you shouldn't expect mayhem, you might find solace, understanding or even amusement reading this. I can't wait for the upcoming prequel!" - **Vera Kabushemeye**

A Reconciliation With Death

Copyright © 2020 by Cody George

ISBN-10: 0578727919

ISBN-13: 978-0578727912

ASIN: B08CT1DTT8

Timeline

Cade & Tawny

March 2011

Wyatt & Gene

September 2012 / January 2019

Lorelei Coffin

June 2012 / March 2019

Joey & Sarah

June 2012 / April 2019

Fran & Corey

June 2012 / July 2019

Table of Contents

Joey & Sarah : *Part One*

Unbeknownst to the architect who created it, the Victoria Family Counseling building would become a hotspot for locals a half-century after its erection. Dark, wooden planks are attached to the plain white walls in a semblance of decorum. They are swollen with small bubbles that burst under the varnish. Tall hedges are well-kept thanks to the property manager who insisted on watering them himself.

A flat roof extends out to create an umbrella for those who are unfortunate enough to be stuck in the rain after a session with one of the many fine psychotherapists that are kept warm and dry inside. The rain had never bothered the locals much before, yet there would always be the obligatory curse to the skies. A shaking fist, balled with mock anger. "How dare it rain on this fine day," someone would say. "I was planning on going to the beach."

The little inconveniences do not matter much anymore, whether it be rain or being bumped by another car. In a general sense, people are more friendly now. To Dr. Sarah Foster, she considered people more *quiet* now.

She, too, considers herself quiet, having experienced much of the event that causes her dayplanner to be filled with little scribbles of notes and names she referred to without end. There is one now, a light-blue mark having smeared the fresh ink. A brand new highlighter with a ruined tip. Again, a little inconvenience that will not influence her day one way or another.

"You're the foster guardian of…" Sarah refers to the blemished name. "Joseph?"

Standing across from her in the center of a dim hallway is an elderly woman whose mouth wrinkles with a stern frown.

Her head bobs a few times in affirmation. "Yes, Joey." She looks to her left in expectation. The child, still in the lobby, is waiting to be called. "I can't get much from him. A word here-or-there, but a conversation has almost never happened."

"You said almost never. Almost never is better than never. What were the events that led to the conversation?"

"Something about, oh, a video game or comic book. Something I don't have much interest in, but my husband does." The woman, who has yet to introduce herself, places a hand over her mouth. She wears bright red lipstick that bleeds over the lines of her lips. Her hair is thin enough that Sarah is able to see through it and to the framed photograph of a serene waterfall.

The doctor smiles and thumbs through two specific sheets of paper for a list of interests. Could be one of these superheroes I've never heard of. Along the way, Sarah finds the woman's signature. "I see. To me, that's hopeful. What's your husband's name and will I have the chance to meet him?"

Ethel pauses. It takes a considerable amount of energy not to break eye contact. "Oh, he—I'd say he doesn't believe in this stuff, but I don't want to offend you." A gulp so hard it visually travels down her throat. "He's more of a 'man up' type of guy, if you know what I mean."

"I do." A mental sigh of exhaustion. "What are some effective ways that I can communicate with Joseph?" There is a blank stare on the old woman's face. She shakes her head with no attempt to reply. "What I mean is, have you had success in attempting alternative methods of communication? Drawing pictures, or…"

"Oh," she laughs. "He loves drawing. Yes, I imagine that'd be fine."

"Do you have any children of your own with autism?"

"No!" Ethel recoils, then catches her tone with a net made of smiles. "'No children' is what I mean. I never had the desire until I was in my late-forties, but I was told that I was unable to conceive. Such a cruel sense of humor God has, but I know it was for a reason."

Sarah's shoulders tense. A recurrent event in her profession is dealing with the trauma of those who are not her clients. Today will be a strange day, she decides. "You believe God has led you to the path of adopting Joseph." There is no answer, so she busies herself by flipping to the last sheet attached to her clipboard. An irrelevant HIPAA agreement that she dutifully studies before changing the subject. "Welp, everything looks good to me."

"Ah, okay," she blinks and wonders if there was ever the possibility of "it" looking bad. "Good! Would you like me to get Joey now?"

"Joey. Does he prefer this name?"

"Seems he doesn't prefer any name. I'll be right back."

Once the woman exits into the attached corridor, Dr. Sarah Foster exhales a blubbering raspberry. The result of an interruption in her morning routine is only now beginning to rear its head. A thrumming pressure sears the inside of her skull, as if a lazy cellist drags their bow along its thickest string.

There is a Keurig in the lobby, she thinks while chewing her thumb. There isn't enough time. I'll just get it la—

Ethel's voice was three decibels higher yet trapped in a whisper.

Look, Joey! It's your new friend!"

Sarah clears her throat and musters the energy to feign enthusiasm. "Hi, Joey." Her voice is kept in a consistent calm during their introduction. "I hope we didn't keep you waiting for long. Were you playing with the toys or reading any of the books?"

The child—who looks a tad young for his supposed age of eleven—wears a pout with an aura that is heavy with depression. He does not look up to meet her eyes, but his lips twitch in response. A small cast to the side. She considers this little gesture promising. Ethel answers for him. "Just watching TV! A little cartoon with doggies. Woof, woof!"

Joey brings his arms to his body when she reaches forward to tickle his sides. It looks like he is trying his damndest not to scream. Sarah jumps to his rescue by tapping the woman's shoulder. This gets her attention and prevents a potential onslaught of non-consensual touch. She wonders how often this happens and decides to add it to an ever-growing list of questions for him.

The door is opened and she stands aside, trying her best to plant a comforting smile on her face. Joey looks up and into the room and quietly inhales a reservoir of air. He keeps his breath held as Ethel walks with him. When they enter the office, he allows himself to exhale.

Two large windows shielded by slotted blinds let in what little light exists during the shallow rainfall. Shelves of bound books offer the only variation in color, pardon a large portrait that hangs above her chair.

Scribbles and splotches, vague faces that are revealed the longer one stares at it. A confusing mess to an adult, but something inspirational for a child.

He keeps his eyes on it during the remainder of their introduction. Sarah throws an occasional question to him, and he does not feel an obligation to respond. His guardian has been removed from the room for a few minutes, only realizing this when he ascertains his surroundings with a brief sweep of the head. Joey returns to the painting.

"Do you like it?" At this point, she is not holding out hope for a response. Sarah joins him in a mutual appreciation. "Every time I look at it, something else pops up."

"Like a face."

She feels her throat tighten and eyes water, but does not look away from the painting. "Yes. Like faces, or, if you look over in that corner," a finger draws an invisible circle. "A puppy or cow."

"Cow, 'cause of the spot in the middle."

Sarah fixes her gaze to him. He makes direct eye-contact without fail. Joey, still standing, wrings his hands. "Why do you feel—please, feel free to sit. There's a carpet, too, in front of the window if you'd like." The boy takes a seat across from her, a circular table the only means of separation between the two. "Why do you feel comfortable enough to talk to me and not your… And not Ethel?"

He bows his head and exhales a hot sigh. His eyes search for an answer, but every time one comes close, the boy lets it go.

"Have you noticed that you hold your breath a lot?"

"Yeah."

"I do that, too." She nods when he perks up. "Yeah, I do. Do you know why?" Joey shakes his head. "It's something called anxiety. Have you heard that word before?"

"Yes, like anxious. I am anxious."

Sarah opens the pages of her clipboard and marks a box, then scribbles a note. "How do you know you're anxious?"

He scrunches his nose for a while, then releases when there is a decision to respond. "Mom told me I'm anxious one time."

"Mom as in Ethel, or mom as in your birth mom?"

"Ethel is not my mom." Joey's posture falters and his gaze floats away. "She's *annoying*."

Sarah coughs up a burst of laughter, then waves at her face as if saying good-bye. "Oh, boy. I shouldn't have laughed. I'm sorry."

"No, it's okay," Joey adjusts his seating and crosses his hands together so that they rest in the center of his lap. "It's okay."

"Okay. So, your birth mom used to say you were anxious?"

"Mhm. I didn't know what it means. I still don't think I know."

"Well, that's okay. I'm here to tell you what it means. Anxiety, or being anxious, is when you feel a lot of stress, or a lot of feeling uncomfortable all at once."

The way he nods is interpreted as understanding. She asks if he is able to relate. "Yes. I am anxious."

"You're anxious right now?" Another nod. "Can you do me a favor? Lower your shoulders for me until you can't lower them anymore." He does so. "Then, uncross your legs and put your hands on your knees.

"How do you feel?" Sarah asks.

Joey nods. "I feel okay. Good, I guess."

"I'm happy to hear that you feel better. Now, every time you feel anxious, I want you to remember how you're sitting." He hears the request but does not respond. "And, Joey, if you ever see me sitting how you were sitting before, let me know right away. Okay?"

"Okay, I will." A tiny seed of responsibility is planted somewhere in his chest. His eyes are a tad more bright.

Sarah pauses to smile while she considers the next phase of her questioning. The pen she holds in her hand feels heavier than before. "Joey," she is slow to start for her sake rather than his. "Can you tell me about when you… When your mom and dad didn't come back?"

That cursed, depressive cloud finds its way back to the boy like a magnet to metal. She looks to the window and opens herself to what little light finds its way in. If Sarah were a plant, she would lay down on the ground and spread her arms out to accept nourishment from the sun. There would be no more questions. Not today, not ever again.

"Hey," Joey says after holding another breath. Sarah returns to reality and uncrosses her legs. His pointer finger drops back to his knee. "Caught you."

The doctor scoffs while grinning. "Yup. Yeah, you got me."

"You were crossing your legs. Thought you were just messing with me. You do it, too."

"Yes, sir."

The air, for a moment, is much cleaner, as if their shared laughter burned away any stagnant bacteria and dispelled the heavy aura that trails him like a shadow.

A plate decorated with pastel flowers is set in front of the young boy while chatter from a television eats away at any peace he wishes he had. From the kitchen, Ethel holds a conversation with her husband. "All I'm saying is, she seemed very sweet!"

"That's their job," Ricky tamps the head of a lit cigarette onto a ceramic ashtray. A glowing screen faces him while he takes up residence in the home's most comfortable seat. Plush under pleather, the arms are torn in the exact spots he rests either arm. "They gotta look sweet, ham it up, talk you up, get your guard down."

"Oh, I don't know about that." The oven door slams. Joey can see her shadow dance along the hanging cabinets, but not her body. A wall separates them.

"Huh?" He tilts his ear to her direction. "What?"

Ethel pops through the threshold. "I said I don't know about that. To be honest, I don't know what the hell they do, but something's gotta give with him." She rarely refers to Joey by name. He slinks in his seat. "Come sit, dinner's ready."

-

Morning arrives when the sun struggles to hoist itself above the horizon. Joey's body, already attuned to the ridiculous schedule his foster parents tend to keep, wakes him up with a gentle nudge. A loud plastic clock hangs on the wall across from him. It reads six-fifty-eight. He has two, maybe three minutes to enjoy the only quiet he will experience today.

He can expect Ethel to knock first, her breathy voice requesting that he stirs to waking life. Not a minute later will Ricky pound twice—always twice—before opening the door. If it is locked, he will shout the boy's full name. "Joseph!"

One more minute, at least.

Uncomfortable white walls are made comfortable by decorating it with as many wall-hangings as possible. Nine-by-nine inch canvases of amateur paintings from when Ethel's church had their short lived activity night. Cut outs from newspapers inform him of insignificant aspects of history he would have been fine to stay oblivious to.

One of his foster fathers, Richard "Ricky" McLeod as stated by the clipping, is to his direct left. A younger version of the irritable man stands with one of his friends. They are both holding onto a large fish of some kind. The names are highlighted in pink.

A few soft knocks. "Joey, sweetie. Joey, you gotta get dressed and meet us out here." She walks away. He knows this because of her oversized slippers that scrape along the wooden floors.

The boy takes a deep breath and throws the covers away before rolling out of bed. He lunges towards the door and reaches for the handle. Only one heavy knock is able to strike the surface before Joey pulls it open. He looks up to his foster father who is already dressed in a navy suit and white tie thrown over a pressed white shirt with a stiff collar.

The expression on Ricky's face, at first, displays genuine confusion, and then, after a moment of consideration, settles into something that resembles being humored. "Out of breath already?"

Joey swallows. He does not know how to respond.

"We gotta exercise you. You like baseball?"

"Sure." This is a lie, but it does not matter to him. A glow enters his heart. Ricky nods once while expressing a flat smile, then walks away with slow steps.

He stands in the doorway with his right hand still on the handle. On the other side of the hall is a small bathroom that holds onto a perpetual scent of artificial strawberries.

-

Joey's eyes squeeze shut while his pastor prays for his congregation. He never believed he would belong to such a group of people. The idea was floated to his birth father once, who shook his head and laughed while eating a bowl of cereal. Captain Crunch, the boy recalls with a growing smile.

He stops himself. There is something about being in a church setting that makes him feel sinful for feeling pleasure. The pensive boy removes his smile and shelves the memory for another time. A certain string of words forces him to tune into the man's speech.

"You know you would not be here to receive the divine word of God today given if circumstances were different. You know you would not *love* your family the same way. The way you show love and receive love, I bet everything, is much more potent and visceral than ever before."

His old friend the cloud sets upon him like a crown atop a king's head.

A hand, large and firm, rests on his left shoulder and squeezes once. Joey peeks through his eyelashes. Ricky keeps his attention to the pastor. Next to him, Ethel is stuck in a continuous loop of nodding and thanking the Lord.

-

Sarah sips on a faux latte pushed out from a rubber nozzle. A strange new machine is welcomed into the lobby with open arms. Her receptionist, a frail redhead also named Sara, is on her second cup. "Did you try the mocha one?"

"No," the doctor examines the contents of her paper cup, the heat of which dares to burn her palm. She places it on the desk and snatches a second, empty cup from a diminishing stack.

"You have to. Please. I swear to God it'll change your life."

Double-cupped, she ventures her second taste. "Honestly, I don't even think I like this one." She shakes her head. The concept of dairy being expelled after being held in some sort of tank does not appeal to her.

Sara clicks her tongue and offers her drink. It looks darker and more frothy. Though it does appeal to Dr. Foster, she declines with a polite shake of the head. "Okay," the girl says. "But you'll be forced to one day."

"Can I see that pen? What do you mean, 'forced'?"

"You'll run out of options soon. There are only four flavors. Plain, vanilla, caramel, mocha. Two styles, a latte or a cappuccino."

Sarah cocks an eyebrow and clicks the pen with her free hand. "Then you'd be plussed to know that a mocha cappuccino is now at the literal bottom of my list. Call me when Joseph Collins arrives."

"You mean McLeod?" Sara checks the sheets when Sarah throws her a heated look. "Ah, right. Yes, ma'am. Will do!"

The girl's tone never fails in its bubbly exterior. There are moments where she wonders what lies beneath, knowing that no one is bereft of trauma and especially so after the last ten years. Sarah could offer her services, but that could mean a breach of some sort of boundary she does not care to cross.

She smiles and thanks her before rounding down the hallway and disappearing into her office.

"I heard you've been more talkative," she says to Joey. He appears to be much more alert than their initial session. "And that's awesome!"

"Thanks." This is said in a mutter, but any progress is progress.

"Why do you think you feel more comfortable speaking now?"

"Um," his eyes widens and he sucks his lips. "Well, I guess, I think I like them. I mean, nothing can replace mom and dad."

Sarah nods. "Is that what they told you?" He confirms with a soft shrug. "I'm glad that you feel safe at home. Is everything alright, though? You're being fed, you're getting enough sleep?"

"The food is weird. Too much salt."

"Are they smokers?" She knows that someone in the household must be. The boy's clothing reeks. Joey nods. "That tends to happen with smokers. They need a lot of salt because they can't taste much of anything. Other than the food, is there anything you want to talk about?"

His eyes fix on a random point in the room. He drops his shoulders and breathes out. "I miss silence."

Sarah jots down a note. "Is your family loud?"

Joey thinks about his answer, then shakes his head. "No more loud than a normal family, I guess. I just…"

The therapist keeps her gaze on him, but switches to another sheet that details what of his past they are aware of. Corroborating stories from police and the remainder of his previous family had given his foster parents a lot to chew on.

"Is this because of… When you were alone?"

"Alone?"

"Alone in your house with your babysitter."

"My nanny. Yeah," he bites his lower lip. His posture returns to stress. "I think so."

She forces a hard swallow. Nothing seems to clear the passage in her throat for her to ask her next question. "Do you want to tell me about it?" The way she phrased her question is considered strange to Joey, who retreats back inside of his own mind to face the memories on a non-verbal battlefield before molding them into words.

Joey & Sarah : *Part Two*

"Do we have time?" He looks for a clock to no avail. She insists that there is and he stretches his arms out before placing both hands on her knees. A deep, cleansing sigh and another pout. "Okay," the syllables are dragged.

"If at any point you feel uncomfortable, please let me know. We will stop talking about it."

There is an emerging conflict inside of the woman as she says this. The stories she has heard from her other clients about the infection caused her to develop an intimate relationship with melatonin, Nyquil—anything that would help during the night. Sarah holds onto the fear that, at some point and possibly sooner than she'd like, there would have to be a means to get her through the day as well. Coffee is no longer cutting it.

The double-cupped latte is hidden in a cubby to her right, where her Coach bag lays above a cache of snacks. White chocolate pretzels and Swedish Fish. Both will become stale within the next week, for her stomach almost never welcomes solids anymore.

Joey inhales a shaky breath. He did not think that they would approach the subject so soon. "I don't know how to start."

Understandable. "What is your nanny's name?" Sarah figures that she will skirt around the matter of his parents for now and close in once he feels a little more at ease. He tells her, but a weight obscures his words into inaudibility. "Did you say… Sorry, I didn't…?"

"Lucy. I'm sorry."

"It's okay, I just didn't hear you. Can you tell me about Lucy?" She receives a blank response, as if someone decided to shut off the kitchen lights while he was in the middle of

cooking.

She witnesses the gears turn inside of his brain.

Movements from his fingers that stretch and contract as a benign

form of procrastination. His left foot moves backwards and his

spine bends. He nods, makes brief eye contact, then looks away.

~*~

The lights in Joey Collins' childhood home were never

raised beyond a specific level; a slider was consistently stuck in

its half-way mark. Tall lamps had been fit in a few corners of the

house, and even slim wicker torches were planted in the

backyard. These were stylistic choices, of course, but had the

dual function of keeping the family calm. Each one of them had

a sensitivity of some kind, whether it be sound, smell, or light.

Joey had always chosen to spend his free time either on the patio or exploring the enclosed space just outside of it. A brown fence made of virgin plastic lumber, their pointed tips reminding the boy of how it must feel to live in a castle. There were two trees on either side of the fence, one inside of his yard and the other on the other. When he stared up at night, as the cicadas hiccupped and smoke from nearby barbecues littered the air, he saw the stars he wished he could grab.

The sound of the sliding glass door being opened stirred him from a simple meditation of staring at the sky. Lucy's voice, inflected with an accent he had never heard before, called for him. Joey did not turn. His bare feet were planted to the earth with wiggling toes that felt the dry soil break under them.

"Would you like to come and sleep?" She asked the child who was only five at the time. "Joseph, please come here."

He turned with a goofy grin, proudly flourishing new teeth that leapt from his gums. Even as a child, his hair was impressive. An orb of small and loose curls packed together like a curious planet. "Mm!"

Lucy and he used to meet twice a week, and every time he considered it a game. She is not his parent, just a silly girl with a strange voice who likes to talk on the cell phone too much.

Her eyebrows raised. On a normal day, she would engage with him on these antics, but the look on her face unsettled him. With a panic in her voice, she asked once more. Lucy gestured with quick, hard movements, and he obliged.

The patter of his dusty feet slapped against the stepping stones that led to the patio. His nanny had left the door open for him and stood aside with patience. Joey crawled into a pair of house sandals and made his way to the kitchen. Lucy was close behind as she dialed, once again, the number that belonged to Earl Collins.

No answer, but he could hear the voicemail message from the tinny speakers. "This is Earl, I'm either with family or asleep. If you'd like to leave a message, I'll—"

Lucy grunted and pocketed her phone. She looked to the boy who stared back with curiosity. "I don't know what to do." This was not directed to him, just at him. "I gotta go. I can't be stuck here all night."

"Mommy, daddy will come back." Joey skews his lips into a cute expression, but she was not amused. The girl found almost nothing funny.

She scratched her left eyebrow for a moment, flakes falling and landing on her oversized t-shirt, and checked the time on the microwave. Two hours late, Lucy shook her head and felt irritation grip the back of her throat. She walked to a drawer and scribbled a note with a dying Sharpie. "Come on," the girl leads Joey to his room.

-

"So," Sarah rolls her tongue on the inside of her cheek. Ridges are torn into the walls. "She left you in bed and went home?"

Joey nods. "I couldn't sleep. I don't know why."

"Do you ever have difficulty falling asleep?"

He looks up and hums. "No, I don't think so. Not back then." She nods with complete empathy. If it weren't rude, she would reach for that disgusting, lukewarm excuse for a latte.

"When you couldn't fall asleep, what did you do?"

"I waited." He shrugs, his tone nonchalant as if to imply there was nothing else he could do. "Sometimes I think I dreamed but I don't remember what."

-

The smell of pan-seared vegetables pushes Sarah into a fugue state in order to recall a memory of her childhood. An elusive memory, at that. Something to do with her father, her head shakes in slow berths. She closes her eyes and relaxes.

She is no longer in her girlfriend's kitchen. The uncomfortable wooden seats that are too tall for her do not exist. A void that first displays as a black screen. Her father's face appears, defined and lucid, suspended with a smile.

Sarah knew this image well as it is always the first to appear. The second, a hand with a gold band on the ring finger. Third, corn on the cob grilled on one side. Fourth…

A plate slides in front of her and she is startled enough to open her eyes. She looks up, smiles, and extends a quiet but genuine thanks. "No problem," Brenda says with a musical lilt. "I thought you said you weren't tired?"

"Me?"

"Yes." She takes her seat at the table. Two glasses of water are untouched with condensation rolling down the side.

Sarah blinks twice and rubs the corner of her eye. "You asked me an hour ago. A lot can change in an hour."

"*I* should be tired," she insists and begins cutting the vegetables with a knife and fork. Bell peppers, onions, cauliflower. "A lot can change in an hour. Sure can! I managed to cook this whole thing."

The devout therapist bites her tongue and reaccesses the response she *wants* to say. Instead, she nods. "And it looks amazing." There is the initial swig from her cup. Sarah wipes the moisture from her hands onto her flannel pajama bottoms.

"This whole Keto thing, I swear to God." Brenda hisses and brings the fork to her mouth. With just olive oil, salt, pepper, and Old Bay, the meal does not contain much flavor at all. Before it enters her mouth, the woman stops to examine her partner. "You really are exhausted, huh?"

Sarah shrugs, her shoulders locked. "I mean, every day my schedule is booked. From the moment I walk into *Victoria*, I have, like, five updates about rescheduling this person and that person. People who show up early, people who email me in the middle of the night..." The fork drops to her plate and she crosses her arms with a huff.

A pause of consideration from Brenda, then a bite. After swallowing, "You're complaining about money?"

She stares her down. "I'm complaining about the absolute mental torment I have to endure."

"What happened between you and your therapist?"

"I still go. Sunday evenings at his house."

Brenda smirks. "Yeah, okay. What, boo? You go to your therapist's house for a one-on-one, then come home and go straight to bed? Just tell me you're cheating on me."

Sarah's hands fling into the air, each finger spread out like an offended umbrella. There is a moment of tension between the two as she renders a response. Brenda waits with her face tilted to the side, one eye kept on her while her lips could be misinterpreted as a smirk.

"Problem?" The woman takes another stab from her pile of vegetables. They are overcooked and somewhat flaccid. Where there should be a crunch, there is, instead, a soft squish. A pepper falls from the prongs and reintroduces itself to its family.

-

Ricky's vehicle reflects the type of person he is: old.

Four tires have not been changed in a decade, as there are only three destinations on his route at any given time. Church, home, Foodsmart—and not always in that order. Today, however, he stores two lunch boxes packed the night before into a flimsy cooler sat by Joey's feet.

"Keep that safe down there," the man requests with a stern voice, as if it held government secrets that would send the general population into dismay and panic. Along their drive, Ricky would ask Joey to make sure it's still tucked between his feet. "It can't go sliding around. What's in there is very important for you and I both."

The boy squeezes the cooler tightly between his heels. Joey is not aware of what is contained inside. He guesses food, but it was just a guess.

The density of trees that fill the space between major roads dwindle until they cross onto a highway. Joey looks out of the window and over a large lake that divides their town from the city. It is a familiar sight, having witnessed it once before as he was carted into the suburbs by Ethel on his first day to their home.

He knows that Ricky is not returning him, as it were, but the discomfort he feels is too real to not acknowledge. "Where are we going?"

"You said you liked baseball." Ricky coughs and feels his lungs rattle like cowbells in a stampede. "Going to a field I looked up on Google. It looks good. Big, well-kept."

Joey looks to the backseat, half-expecting a pair of baseball bats. The old man intuits his confusion and states that everything they need is in the trunk. "I wish the radio in this thing worked," he taps the dim screen. "I always imagined a radio."

-

The smart watch that hugs Sarah's wrist vibrates and a notification fades in. She lifts herself from her chair, out of her office, and calls for Joey. There is not enough energy in her body to smile. Ethel kisses him on the hand and sends him off. She remains seated while doing so, ostensibly finding the routine of therapy a little more familiar now.

Both Joey and his therapist catch up. They run through their feelings for the past week and any exciting events that may have happened. "Ricky took me to the ballpark in the city. We had ham and cheese and soda."

A scratch on her notepad. "That sounds very fun. What kind of bread was it on?" She pauses and furrows her brow. What kind of *bread*?

"White." Even Joey seems to pick up on this fumble. "Never had soda before. Just different teas."

Sarah prevents herself from asking what kind of soda. Irrelevant! Stick to the agenda.

She listens as he details his morning and claims that his foster father plans on fixing the car radio with him. "That sounds like fun. Have you ever done anything like that before?"

A shake of the head. "Does it interest you, to get your hands dirty and see something work again?"

"Yeah. I didn't think about it like that."

"Well," the therapist straightens her posture. "I think you'd be excellent at it. No, really. You're very attentive, you remember fine details. When you were telling me about Lucy," she double checks the name. "You brought up a lot of interesting details that, at least in my career, not a lot of children would care to remember."

Joey almost smiles. His eyes are fixed to her nose, just a few degrees from her eyes. His silence is clean and eager, so she continues. "A lot of people I work with, even older people, don't remember what they ate the last day."

"Really?" A crack of a smirk, but he bites his lip to hide it. At least he finds the anecdote humorous. She is curious to unlock his sense of humor.

"Yes, really. What else do you remember about that night?"

"You don't wear nail… Nail stuff." He brings up his hand and points at his naked cuticles. "Like me, but I'm not a girl, so I don't have to, but you are and you don't."

For the first time this week, there is a genuine expression on her face. "That's strange, isn't it?" He nods. "Why do you think nail polish is just for girls?"

Joey cocks his head. "Because I've only seen it on girls?" Emotion in his voice. Don't fuck it up.

She refrains from speaking to deliberate as to which route she should take. Children nowadays are much more open to the idea of gender politics. Should she divert and inform him, taking up precious time?

"What if I told you," Sarah starts. "That I'm not wearing nail polish because… Because it tastes bad?" He frowns and his head twitches to the side, then giggles. A feeling of bliss washes over her face, then chest. She is reminded as to why she prefers working with children.

"It *tastes* bad?"

"Remember when we talked about anxiety? Yeah, well, in addition to me crossing my legs and all of that, I also like to bite my nails. Do you bite your nails?"

"Um, no. That sounds gross."

There's no reason to be offended, she thinks while scratching her nose. He's right, after all. "It is, and it's more gross with nail polish. There would be little flecks of color in my teeth all day and no one would tell me."

The boy pauses and shifts in his seat. He crosses his hands. "If it's gross and you don't want to do it, then—wait, you should keep using the nail polish. If it tastes bad then you won't want to bite them, so…"

Sarah lifts up her thumb from her clipboard and examines it. Her length of her right thumb nail does not match its accomplice. The thought of acrylics does not appeal to her, either, though Brenda spends a lot of time working on her own while sat in front of the news.

It's possible I'm projecting, the therapist considers. I resent her, so I resent what is associated with her.

She returns to reality as if a light dimmer was moved from its half-way mark. "I think you're right. See? You notice all of the fine details we adults don't bother with."

"I think—" he hesitates to finish his thought. A helpful word of encouragement from his therapist nudges him in the right direction. "Yes, I am proud of that."

"Good, you should be, and it's going to help us out a lot when we talk about what caused you to be here." The child frowns. "I believe, Joey, that everything happens for a reason, even the painful stuff."

You know you would not be here to receive the divine word of God today given if circumstances were different.

He coughs out, "Do you believe in God?"

"Oh!" Sarah stammers. "I—I mean, I…" She calms herself down with a sharp exhale. "I don't feel comfortable enough to answer that, Joey."

"What? Why not?"

Here we go. "That's a topic that is difficult for me to talk about. Keep in mind, if you ever feel uncomfortable about something, you can let me know and—"

"But I told you about Lucy," Joey pouts. Either leg crosses over one another. "And I have to talk about mom and dad, so it doesn't make sense that..."

Sarah initiates a moment of relaxation by practicing her own advice. One deep breath, then lowered shoulders. Joey follows suit after a moment of reluctance. When they are both at an equilibrium, she checks her watch. Forty more minutes.

-

The covers are pulled from Sarah's body and are forced into a bundle over Brenda. Her eyes open with a gentle pull, but an unfamiliar pressure in her neck and head prevents her from moving. She stares at the wall, as there is nothing else she can do.

Her mouth wants to open to scream but her jaw is closing in, tighter and tighter, until it feels as if each tooth will shatter under the force. She wished that Brenda cared enough to cuddle her in the way Val once did.

Something else is on the bed with them, a quadrupedal shadow that lanks to-and-fro with egregious dips until it lingers in front of Sarah's face. A dark form with unpronounced features that eventually focus into clear definition. She feels her mouth open, though the force of which is equated to a crowbar peeling an elevator door open.

A cat, and though it is not a stranger, it is unwelcomed.

The same green eyes hold the exact intelligence it had almost a decade ago. It should have been dead and buried under a pile of trash somewhere in a barge floating along the sea.

Though she regains her faculties, the creature is unmoving. A statue that represents too much to process. When she rolls onto her back after a massive effort, she can see how the cat transfers its gaze to the woman next to her. Brenda, and not Val? Its eyes shift back to Sarah and portray an emotion that is not betrayal, but incredulousness. Brenda and not Val?

Really?

The first thing Sarah manages to say—with each syllable sticking to the roof of her mouth is, "I know, she sucks."

Brenda takes in a shallow inhale through her nose. "Talking about me?" Lucidity falls away, and Sarah remains silent until she can hear the peaceful snores ripple through the room. She can live without the comforter, without comfort. It is yet another little inconvenience that does not mean much

anymore.

Joey & Sarah : *Part Three*

The cat should be gone by now yet the terrible specter remains for another few minutes until Sarah can no longer consider herself tired. She is not rested by any means, and is instead wired from adrenaline that increases a steady supply to her veins the longer she is forced to stare at the vision of her ex-girlfriend's dead cat.

That bastard caused all of this, the woman clenches her jaw and refuses to acknowledge a sharp pain in the right side of her neck. It forced me into a situation where I had to experience loss and to grieve, where I had to restart my life and it led me to share a bed with Brenda from Whole Foods.

Brenda from *Whole Foods.*

By all accounts, she would rather be alone. In all truth, Sarah has no idea what it means to be alone anymore.

Communities are thriving after the infection and whatever losses the country suffered only helps to bind the remaining population.

She is already trapped in emotional debt, a sinkhole collapsing under the weight of runoff from daily storms.

Perhaps this relationship serves a purpose, one she is not ready to admit but comes close every time Brenda forces eye contact and with every instance of inerudite presumption towards the things that interest her.

"Painting is pointless unless you plan to get good enough to sell what you create." This was said after Sarah helped ship a purchase from Brenda's online resale store.

She blinks when a dry sting attacks her eyes then adjusts the pillow with a soft jerk. When her anxious thoughts dissipate, she notices the cat no longer exists. There is no third presence in the room and the exhausted woman is hard-pressed to even sense a second.

A slim book held by an over-invested Joey Collins is being scoured through for the second time. The cover displays a glowing double-helix laid on top of an ominous color scheme.

When he visited an upscale thrift store with Ethel the day before, he dropped the copy into their cart.

"*Slave Species of the Gods?*" Her tone expressed concern. She looked to her new son and then to the object that interested him the most out of everything in the consignment shop. "You really want to read this?"

"I think so." He knew his answer, yet played coy. Joey watched as she thumbed through each page and finished with a scoff birthed from uncomfortable disbelief. The book hung in her hand like an inimitable weight.

"Can you even pronounce half these words?" A wash of embarrassment blushes his face. "Okay. Alright, we'll get it." It was thrown on top of a floral nightgown with a blue tag.

As he passes through its mid-point, the boy shakes his head and tosses onto his pillow. The concept of God has plagued him for a week. People claim there is a man in the sky, or an invisible force made of love, and now a collective of aliens.

He wonders if there will always be disagreement or if at some point in history will everyone come to a decision.

Ricky and Ethel stand on the side of an ancient man living in the clouds yet she shames him for reading fiction about magical children and talking owls.

-

"Thanks for getting my coffee today," Sarah stretches her arms and embraces a day that is warmer than usual. When she retracts, her elbow strikes a rusted metal table she and her guest claimed. The sole reason her coffee does not spill is the fact her barista shorted her on milk. In spite of this, there is a beautiful flower painted on the surface from an art form she could only appreciate from afar. A woman sitting adjacent to her keeps her eyebrows cocked to the sky as if in warning. "Whew. Almost ruined it."

Patricia Foster blinks in a triplet. "Aren't you going to take a picture?" There is an obligation for the daughter to take out her phone now. Sarah looks at her, forces a smile, and takes a blurry photo that no one would ever see. For posterity, one more is taken to convince her mother that she cares.

"Looks better than what we have at work."

"My office has a Keurig," the aging woman brings a hot tea to her lips. Steam fogs a pair of designer sunglasses that never dared to disrespect her by being smudged.

Sarah rips open a green packet of sugar substitute. A small, white mound lays on top of the latte art. It seems sacrilegious to defile the drink but the espresso used in her mother's favorite cafe is famously bitter. "We have one too, but Tess put in a request for one of those… Oh, I don't know. You press a button and get some goop that is pretending to be coffee."

"Goop." Patricia smirks. The most peculiar things amuses her. It has always been difficult to keep track of how her humor shifted week-by-week. "Well, I'm glad you like this place. I remember when it was that God-awful pizza place."

"More like flatbreads. Yeah, terrible. Only a little—"

"Little, little *sprinkles* of cheese. What's wrong with the Keurig?"

Sarah prepares herself to defend the trusty machine. It had never steered her wrong, yet it is her office who decided on betrayal. "Nothing at all. We take good care of it. Descale it regularly." The sleek appliance was a gift from Patricia during the first week of living in a new apartment.

"Who did you say ordered that thing?"

"Tess. Kroner."

A blank stare falls away to invite in a suspicious look. "The one whose fiance was bit."

Sarah knows that her tone will come across as metallic but does not deny herself the pleasure of making the entitled woman feel uncomfortable. "It was her brother." She watches her mother nod and return to her tea with a lazy shrug lifting her left shoulder. The woman was not bothered in any way.

One courtesy sip. A brief inhale that wet the center of her lips and drew over her tongue like sheer curtains in an attempt to block out the sun.

Patricia had always clung onto some semblance of her bad habits she claimed no longer affected her. No matter how long the two will sit at this rickety metal table, the cup will never be empty even after spending an extra seventy-five cents on a tablespoon of local honey. The woman did not stir the tea and instead let the amber inclusion rest in a congealed pool at the bottom of the tempered ceramic mug.

"That's right. I don't think I ever knew his name. Well, that's sad, isn't it?"

"Yeah." Sarah makes an effort to put a dent into her latte. Without realizing it, their amicable outing became something of a competition. The Stevia does not help the flavor.

"At least we were lucky." Patricia brings the lip of the cup to her mouth, peers over and to her daughter, then draws in a slow and quiet sip. Sarah's cheeks burn in expectation for the next part of her mother's sentiment. "Oh, don't give me that look. You know what I mean."

"No," she keeps her eyes pinned forward. "I don't."

Her head pivots in a loose tilt and from behind the sunglasses were two empty bullets painted with too-much mascara. "Sarah. We didn't suffer any losses from *real* family. Again with that look!" There is a stale laugh before Patricia leans back into her seat. "You knew her for a year."

Though it was nine months, Sarah considers one year enough time to create a strong relationship with someone, anyone. Her throat tightens and an internal conflict builds while she debates saying these exact words out loud.

The molten heat in her eyes dies down and is replaced with cool, malleable ingots. She pries her gaze away from the woman and plants it to the street behind them.

A fragile but cute dog hangs to an elderly gentleman's side. The man wears a tweed jacket and well-fitting navy pants regardless of the heat. His demeanor insists that he feels he deserves to be wherever he decides to go. With his chin held steady and a few degrees above straight, it is a wonder that he finds patience in walking his pet instead of hiring another to do it for him. Unless, of course, there is genuine love.

Or, and not unlike a large portion of the population, he chose to purchase the pet in recent years as a means of superstitious protection. A silly conspiracy shared by those who belong to egregious social classes. Keep it close, Sarah enters a mental dialog with the man as he moves behind her and disappears into her blind spot. Just make sure you at least pet the damn thing every once in a while.

-

Bright letters that were cut from felt in haste are plastered along the wall of a room full of metal chairs, metal tables, and metal bars welded to the windows: *MAKE YOUR DAY AWESOME!*

Joey's new homeroom teacher sits on the other side of a rectangular desk with her nameplate and a paper towel covering slices of a green apple. Moisture bleeds through the material and clings to the fruit that browns faster the longer the discussion lasts.

To his right is Ethel, who keeps straightening her pants in obvious discomfort. The teacher, Ms. Boone, reads off a curriculum. Her voice is hoarse by genetics, with a twinge of a Southern accent lilting every few syllables. She makes an effort to bounce eye contact between the boy and his foster mother.

"And," she blinks once. Long, caked eyelashes bat with so much strength, Joey can imagine the sound. "At the end of the day, we all like to wind down with some light readin'. I do want to ask you somethin', just so there ain't gonna be any surprises later on."

Ethel straightens her posture. "Me? Oh, alright."

"I'm aware you found us through *New Cross*, a wonderful church with a delightful congregation and—oh, that *choir*. Y'all should know Pastor Dave is my hero and I trust that man with my life!" Laughter that is genuine only to her, but when Ethel joins it turns artificial. Ms. Boone clears her throat, as if the effort is going to be enough to smooth out her timbre. "Yes, well, you should already know that we incorporate the Bible and the word of our Lord into class, into what we teach."

"Pastor Dave and Margie told me all about this place. It seems lovely. Perfect for what we want for him."

"Oh, good!" She tilts her head, initiates a too-bright grin, and leans forward to impose over Joey and his silence. "Does that sound good to you, too, Joseph?"

He opens his mouth to ask, Why would God let my parents be killed?

Instead, his lips hang apart and twist into a courteous smile.

Why would God let all of those other kids' parents get killed, too?

—

Friday felt like a Friday to both Joey and Sarah as they occupy the same space but find it difficult to speak with each other in any genuine sense.

They are both sitting on a plush carpet, staring out of a window that invites in a wonderful view of the parking lot. Trees sway with an innocuous wind and, as the therapist rattles off question-after-question, watching the movements provides something of a meditation for the young boy. She joins him after rubbing the back of her neck until it glows red.

"It's nice out," Sarah decompresses into a crossed-leg Yoga pose her mother would know the name of.

"It's going to rain."

"Yeah, I think you're right, but I love the rain." Her face turns to him just enough to ascertain his expression. A little more life than before.

He shrugs, his energy low. "It's always raining. I just want there to be sun so I can go out to the park."

"Have you asked Ricky to take you?" There is a pause long enough that Sarah becomes concerned. A genuine, deep empathic response that is not an obligation and not a persona for the sake of a child. "Joey? Is Ricky okay?"

"He's okay." He throws a sigh and loosens his muscles. "He's, um, a little sick. He's old, so, um, it happens."

She nods. "Does it make you feel scared that you're going to lose him?"

There is no hesitation. "Yes." A veil of tears condenses in his eyes like low-hanging fog intent on obscuring his vision.

Joey continues to watch the empty parking lot, never dissuaded from the fact that no animals can be seen let alone cars or people. His therapist weighs each response that floats in her skull. She repositions herself next to him. His face shakes from holding in emotions related to the security of having a home.

With a watchful eye, Sarah remains still. She hopes that her presence is enough to make him feel comfortable, even if he finds it difficult to verbalize whether or not it is the case. She, too, stares out of the window and is reminded of Val's cat and how it used to guard over the apartment with a watchful eye and a lethargic swing of the tail.

"You know," her voice drops in volume. "I lost someone because of it, too." He rips a long inhale and holds it in his lungs. The woman's advice did not matter to him now. "My girlfriend. She was going to propose to me."

He listens, and Sarah is grateful. The next sentence coats her tongue like Ipecac. "She had a cat." Joey exhales when he feels his lungs ache but she misinterprets this as a response. "Yeah. I know."

"I hate cats."

She laughs. "I understand. Trust me. I never liked them too much before, and now…"

"Whenever I see a cat I get so… I get so anxious." Joey turns his head but looks right past her. "I remember the police shooting them."

This is a heavy topic she is not ready for, but she resolves to pardon her own emotions for the sake of his progress. The *client's* progress, she reminds herself. "Yes. I remember that, too. It was scary."

He shifts his shoulders in a way that dismisses the chosen word. "If I had a gun…"

Sarah flushes with an astringent chill. "What do you think you would do if you had one?" Joey pauses to assess the possibility, then shakes his head. He begins to speak, fumbles a word, then lets it go. "What did you want to say?"

"No," he leaks a pathetic sigh. She catches him staring at the palms of his hands. "Just no. I couldn't."

"Couldn't—couldn't use it?"

"Couldn't..." His lungs fill with stinging air. The boy closes his eyes and wobbles.

She examines him and drags the clipboard from her last position. As the pen strikes the paper with a final flourish of a word, Joey groans. "What's on your mind?" Sarah wants to reach out and comfort him but stops her hands in its tracks.

"Lucy."

~*~

Even while he was alone in his home, the modern yet creaky home felt bloated with the presence of others. Fingers from tree branches scraped the exterior. Shadows cast from orange streetlights sprinted across his window and distorted the emptiness that surrounded him. A pair of voices that belonged to his neighbors were louder than usual and had entered his space as if they sat in the living room.

Another familiar sound appeared while sobs were stifled with a blanket he balled in either fist. He pictured a vehicle in his mind's eye: white and tarnished with dry-rotted tires. Colorful stickers from a handful of music venues pasted to the rear window. On a typical day when the brakes on Lucy's car squealed before coming to a rest in the driveway, some obscure and vocal-driven music would alert the family before she could ever knock at the door.

The vehicle rattled and squealed as usual, yet there was no music to accompany it. There was a pop from the door that opened but no slam to insist it had closed.

Adrenaline ran through his body, a strange and icky feeling for the child who wanted nothing more but to sleep with the comfort of knowing his parents were in the adjacent room. Heavy blackout curtains were withdrawn and he poked his head between them to examine the outside. The car was off and just as he expected, the door was left open. A crumpled bag and plastic cup had been abandoned on the asphalt, kicked out of the vehicle with disrespect to the property.

From within the living room the front door slammed and Joey whipped his head to inspect his own. It's locked, he reminded himself. He wondered, however, if he needed to meet up with Lucy because something seemed very wrong.

She was always careful to clean up any mess she made while sitting for him. Sticky rings of coffee on the granite counters, crumbs from snacks they bought for her. The boy turned back to the window, stretched on his toes, just to double-check that what he had witnessed was correct.

Lucy's voice piped up and whined into her cell phone. It became louder and more frantic until she knocked in a rapid triplet. Joey did not waste any time letting her in.

She dove in with the device to her ear and spun to shut the door. Her voice was low when she said, "G-go lay down and get really comfy." He frowned and looked to his bed. The blanket had been thrown off of the bed and a pillow fell with it. Lucy shoved two fingers into his shoulder and ordered him once more *sans* saccharine.

His lower lip inflated with a pout and slinked to his bed. Feeling as if she had somehow wronged him, Lucy straightened his comforter and aligned each of his three pillows until the young boy was tucked in and safe. He could see her face as she loomed over him.

The girl had never been kind to her body, especially when it came to giving it a proper amount of sleep. Her two shifts with him were five in the afternoon to midnight on Wednesdays, and seven to one in the morning on Saturdays. Despite this, Lucy had never looked tired. Her energy, if anything, seemed to increase the closer it became time for her to go home.

A splay of salty dew, untethered by friction of her glossy skin, rolled down her forehead and collected on the tip of her nose. "Just stay here," Lucy breathed. The odor was awful, like sweet decay. "And don't move until… Until your mom and dad come home. I'm—I called someone to pick me up, so I'm going to…"

She watched over him, swayed in weakness, and blinked before leaving the room.

Even though his nanny happened to be just fifteen feet from him, Joey was overwhelmed with the knowledge that he was alone. Another door was shut and he recognized it as the hall bathroom, since it always stuck and needed to be pulled with much more strength than any other. As he stared at the ceiling, he could hear her cry.

She had a shortness of breath, a coughing fit, and then whined for so long he could not understand how the girl did not run out of oxygen. A bang, to which he jolted in response and brought the blanket back up to his mouth. He felt sweat form on his head as well and hoped he had not contracted whatever sickness Lucy had.

A scrape was followed by the shattering of something small. Joey squeezed his eyes shut and remembered the layout of the bathroom. A toothbrush holder shaped like an elephant. He felt sad because he liked the novelty a lot more than his father expected when he brought it home nearly a year prior.

His breath began to shake when he considered a depressing, entirely possible reality.

Joey imagined his mother entering first, then his father. They would hear a strange sound coming from the bathroom and decide to inspect the scene for themselves. Lucy would rush out, sick and angry, and maybe even hurt them if she was scared. If anything, she could vomit on them and ruin his mother's black dress with the low-cut. He would be blamed for not calling to alert the two that something was amiss. "You should have told us," Earl would scold him and rub his forehead in the way he often did when upset. "We would have come right over, and now she's sick and we have to pay for her hospital bills."

The boy felt his muscles wind into tight knots and rushed out of the room with damp feet patting the floor under him. He skid when he approached the bathroom and hesitated before knocking.

He had expected the girl to tell him to go away. Instead, he received a shout and another bout of thrashing against the flimsy door. It rocked on its hinges with each blow. Joey backed away, not even able to recognize who was on the other side. One continuous scream was held until her voice curdled and cracked.

For a brief second, there was a pause, as if he had entered the eye of a storm wherein peace is but an illusion. This ended when he whimpered.

Lucy resolved to use her entire body weight. He watched the door separate from the frame and was able to see the light from within. She held the push while her feet scraped along the floor but eventually her knees gave away. The girl collapsed against the door, scrambled back up, and tried again.

Red light trickled into the home through the cracks of its thick curtains. A thrum of color and an abrasive siren.

-

Sarah sucks on her teeth and stares at the boy. His cheeks are glossed with tears, but he does not react with fear or sadness. There is just an obligation to retell the events as insisted by Ethel and, later, Ricky.

When he wills himself to look at his therapist in the eyes, she feels her heart skip a beat. "You"—she has never felt words have any less meaning—"said you couldn't shoot Lucy."

"Yeah."

"That means you found a gun?"

"No," he frowns. "I don't think we have one."

Relief enters her soul. One less terrible image to have. "I understand now. Do you remember what… Of course you remember. Would you like to tell me?"

Joey shrugs and exhales a sharp breath. He reels his legs to his chest and wraps his arms around his knees. "Um, the ambulance came and took her."

"Was she still angry?" He shakes his head. "They found her dead?" She might as well use the correct vernacular. After these few weeks together, Sarah realized, and appreciated, the fact that he doesn't like when she infantalizes him.

"Mm, yeah. Her heart stopped."

"Yep. I heard they did that." Sarah brings a hand to her mouth and relives the moments with lucidity as if she had actually been there with him. "And then, according to the, erm, papers I have, the police found your parents a few days later. The same way, too, a heart attack." She lets him absorb this. "Did it make you feel better when you found out they were together when it happened?"

Joey can not deny that it did. She nods and continues. "And does it make you feel, I guess, *happier* that they were found with their heart stopped and not… You know, injured, or—like, remember when the police were out shooting the cats?" He nods, irritated. She decided not to continue with her implication.

Her client shows his discomfort with a tightly-wound posture, so she reminds him to relax and breathe. After a minute break, too short to forget but long enough to process, Sarah reiterates her question. "Do you find relief in knowing that they didn't hurt anyone before they died?"

The boy bites the tip of his tongue until the resting flavor of his mouth changes to remind him of frayed wires. "I am glad I didn't get hurt."

There is an audible sigh that escapes Dr. Sarah Foster's pressed lips as she reaches for her clipboard. It is as if her fingers are controlled by a puppet master that guides her movements by the logic of her career's imperative. She can imagine a voice in her ear and an invisible entity on her shoulder leaning forward to whisper: "Not so cute anymore, huh?"

Wyatt & Gene : *Part One*

"Are there actually bullets in that thing?" An exasperated college-aged man asked while clutching an unimpressive knife in his right hand and the loop of a leather leash in his left. Several feet in front of him was an intruder who did not belong anywhere near Wyatt's home.

A snub-nose revolver was pointed at his head. His companion, a straight-nosed and patient dog, was becoming restless as the two had spent too much time talking and not enough time playing with him. Jekyll craned its head to Wyatt and huffed. The invader grinned, as if playing a game he knew he could win.

The gun rotated from the young man and to a framed picture of a family that was neither of theirs. One squeeze, bereft of hesitancy or consideration of any kind, and the frame fell. Glimmering dust scattered on the carpeted floor. The man, a grey headed individual with stubble and dilated pupils, responded with, "What? You asked if I had bullets."

Wyatt hushed his dog whose tongue hung with heavy panting. Whining paired with heavy strings of saliva. "I mean," he bent his knees enough so it was easier to scratch behind Jekyll's pointed ears. "You had *a* bullet. I could see that you had one single bullet, and you wasted it on a picture of my roommate's parents."

The man sucked on his teeth. His head bobbed a few times. "You think I came here with just one bullet?" His voice was as smooth as coconut oil, his tone just as slick. He cocked the weapon and trained it on the dog.

"Don't do that," Wyatt warned. His fingers wrapped tighter around the handle of a paring knife retrieved from a wooden block somewhere in his kitchen. "I know there's nothing in there, but, still. Don't do that. It's really rude."

"You know what? You're right," the man stepped forward and caused Jekyll to jerk himself into a heel. There was hesitation from the intruder, and then a smirk to overcompensate. "Don't want to hurt your dog, I just need him for something."

Wyatt shook his head, clearly humored by the gall. A gentle pull on the lead was enough for the dog to sit at ease. The man slowed his pace when the two refused to move and raised the gun to intimidate both. "Just," he said through a swallow. His fingers massaged the butt of the pistol. "Give me the damn dog."

"What? No. Plus, I've had him for five years, so even if you kill me and take him, there's no way he's going to respond to you."

"Well, what's his name?"

"What's *your* name?"

The intruder scowled and licked his lips. The house was not as hot as the other homes for he still had working air conditioning. Despite this, dark stains had set into the grey individual's underarms within the time of him walking through the front door unannounced. "Kevin."

"Cool. I'm Wyatt, but you don't get to know my dog's name."

"Fido?" He jested, the gun heavy in his hand. "Max?" His eyes darted from the young man to the dog in hopes that one of the names would register. "Sparky?"

"I'll give you a hint."

Kevin furrowed his brow. He drank in the strange demeanor of the kid—relaxed, for the most part, and with an attitude of someone he would have beat the shit out of in high school. "Really?"

"One hint, one chance. You can keep pointing the gun at me, if you'd like. I don't mind. I can clearly see that it's empty."

Wyatt had successfully called the man's bluff. The single bullet left in the chamber had been wasted in a futile attempt to bully him. The dog seemed well-trained, Kevin thought. Or, trained enough to attack me at the drop of a hat.

With a smack of the lips, the revolver finds a new home in a deep pocket. One-by-one, the knuckle of each finger was cracked. "I answer it right, and you'll hand him over?"

"Sure, but I have another question before all of that. Seriously," he added. "A genuine question." There was a moment of contemplation, but the man nodded to initiate the new phase of their dialog. "What do you hope will be accomplished by stealing my dog?"

Kevin scoffed then paused to examine the man opposite him. "Really? You gotta know by now, kid. Why else would you keep feeding and walking it?"

"You've seen me walking my dog?"

The man's face blanched. "Well," his words were slow. "You must. It smells—you know, *not* like shit in here."

"Fair enough." A nod from Wyatt who then looked to his companion with an assured smile. Even through all of this, Jekyll's schedule was never altered. "And that's also kind of a compliment. Are you ready, Kevin?"

He narrowed his eyes at the sound of his own name. "Sure. Okay."

"The name is pulled from a book written in the eighteen-hundreds."

He shook his head, grimaced, and showed his teeth. It was painful to watch the man run through a mental archive of every book he had ever known, especially when they were so recently rendered as irrelevant. "Ah, boy," Kevin lifted his hands in a gesticulation that insisted that he was thinking. His eyes floated to the dog.

The left side of its face was a lighter color than the right. The ears, stiff triangles, were the same size. No tag, but there was a collar: an aged purple rope that looked repurposed or perhaps just well-worn. He returned to its face and dropped his hands. "Dr. Jekyll and Mr. Hyde?"

Wyatt's nostrils flared when his dog perked up at the sound of his name. A victorious whoop came from Kevin as he celebrated with a fist pump. "Oh, shit," He chortled. "I'm right. Look at your face, I know it. Man, oh, man."

Unperturbed, "How did you know that I still walk my dog?"

"What?" Kevin's laughter dripped away until there was nothing left. "What do you mean? I thought we covered that."

The young man pointed his thumb to a patio door that was attached to the living room where they both idled. "I have a backyard. I could just let him out and he'd go potty with or without me."

There was no going back. "So, why don't you? No, you know what? You're procrastinating." Kevin's hand extended and his fingers flapped inwards several times.

A slow inhale was brought into Wyatt's nose and had mutated into a sigh. "You have more people waiting for you." The intruder's silence, pardon a crisp scoff, was affirmation. "Which house are you all posted in? One of the big ones, I'd guess. That blue one with the gnomes?"

Another bout of quiet consideration before Kevin ventured to speak. "They all know I'm here, so just give up the dog. Don't make this hard."

"But you don't have AC or water. Right?"

"We have some water." He didn't know why he was replying. "Jugs."

Wyatt nodded. "Weapons, too. No doubt, but you probably don't have enough ammunition to spend willy-nilly.

They let you have one bullet just in case I killed you, which means *I* would have one—"

"Why are you talking so much?" He almost reached for the gun cozied up in his pocket as if it were a viable means of defense.

"Because you don't actually want to kill me or currently have the means to, so, that means that I can talk for however long I want."

With frustration built in his chest that channeled through his legs, Kevin lunged forward. His fingers were outstretched, maybe with the intention of strangling or grabbing either of them. With a simple motion, Wyatt raised the knife and backed away with Jekyll at his ankle. The man was prevented from closing any more distance.

The boy and his dog had breached the kitchen with this movement—the coarse sound of his dog's nails scraping against the tile flooring heightened the intruder's annoyance.

Kevin rubbed his lips with one of his unwashed hands. "You're really going to stab me? With that little thing, you think you can kill me?"

"I don't want to find out." A brief pause, then he rolled his eyes. "But, probably. It *is* a knife."

Either man stared each other down and Jekyll became more suspicious over time. The gentle pull on his leash was not enough for him to calm down.

The unarmed individual raised his hands and straightened his posture. For a moment, he appeared less threatening; a middle-aged man wearing flannel and his age in the form of slender creases upon his forehead watched the young man create distance. It was true that Kevin did not mean harm to anybody and he was becoming tired of playing the villain. He smiled at the dog who stopped panting and shut its mouth a second later. There was a question as to whether or not the animal was smiling back.

"So, you named him, what, Dr. Jekyll because of his face? That's cute. I did the same thing with my old cat. I mean, not *exactly* the same thing, but..."

Wyatt raised his chin and kept his focus on him. They were only three, maybe four feet apart—enough space to try again with a higher probability of success. "Are you about to tell me a sob story?"

"Maybe. It's only a sob story if you cry." No objections. "My cat, uh, Nemo." He wiggled his left fingers. "No paw, just a little nub."

"Twenty-five percent less chance he'd scratch you."

"She was a girl, actually. I didn't know any other cool names that made sense."

Without hesitation, "Twenty-five percent less chance *she'd* scratch you, then."

Kevin chuckled. He scratched the crown of his head with the same fingers he used to impersonate his cat. The innocuous movement sent Jekyll into alert mode and Wyatt did not command him to stand down. "Look, kid. Looks like we found some common ground here—"

"Only because you decided it was common." Wyatt dropped the leash and it fell into a loose bundle on the ground. The man flinched, but Jekyll remained still. "How many of you are in that weird gnome house?"

"A lot." The man smiled, then shrugged. His gaze became more gentle. "A few." He could not help but refer to the animal between each truncation.

"How many dogs are there?"

He grunted in exasperation. "None, man. That's why we need yours."

"Why?"

"Because…" For the first time, Kevin dared to look away. When he turned back to face Wyatt, he was somewhat surprised that no attempt on his life was made. "Because it keeps them away." The young man did not look convinced. "It's true. I… I heard it from one of the other guys, but it makes sense. Right?"

Wyatt shook his head and relaxed on his right hip. "No, not at all. Why would it?"

Kevin bit the corner of his bottom lip and began to feel a trickle of regret. It formed like morning dew on his lungs. He feigned confidence. "Because cats did this," he started, as if his explanation was obvious. "And… Cats hate dogs, so…"

"What happens if the cops come back and sweep this area again? What if, whenever they decide to lift the quarantine, they figure out you guys killed me or stole my dog or… You know? This—all of this—isn't permanent, but your actions are."

Wind struggled between the grey man's clogged nostrils. There was a vague whistle from one. "I'm just trying to survive, man." His jaw hardly moved as he spoke. "I'm just trying to get through this, same as you are."

A hum from Wyatt. His posture softened. "Then stay here." Kevin could not decide whether this offer was serious or made to patronize him. "I'm serious. My roommate evacuated with his—erm, with them." He pointed to the broken picture. "There's food here, a ton of bottled water, and a back-up generator with, like, ten gallons of gas standing by. Apparently having a dog is important to you, too."

Kevin nodded for a while, his eyes distant. To his chagrin, he could actually imagine himself being roommates with this kid. He was already debating between two theme songs. "Yeah, that's funny. I'm not able to just leave them, you know? I developed... I've *bonded* with them. Killed infected with them, so I can't just abandon what we made together. Plus, they know where I am and they'd come and find me."

"That's a good point. Why can't we work as a team, then? We can combine our resources, work together. You know, all that jazz?"

The man placed both hands on the back of his neck and flexed. "I don't know. I don't know." The idea was tempting in theory. A scenario ran through Kevin's mind in which his group accepted the idea with open arms and, somehow, they would thrive because of it. There was no reason he could think of that would challenge their potential future.

"Well," Wyatt crouched down and ran his fingers through the tufting around Jekyll's neck. The dog responded with a heavy pant. "Do you know someone who would know?"

-

A two-story blue house with white shutters and decaying shingles sat at an intersection. It boasted an impressive front yard and, even though it was bereft of foliage, would be a picture-perfect location for a family to settle down and allow their dog to run, play, and potty.

Wyatt never knew who occupied the house before quarantine but always held a pearl of jealousy for whomever the lucky denizens were. He resented the fact that they chose garden gnomes as decoration. Obtrusively colorful and useless guardians stood an inch-deep into moist soil, their dumb and vapid faces had always irritated him whenever he passed by with Jeykll while enjoying their otherwise pleasant walks.

He was led to the very house by Kevin, whose body brimmed with nervous energy. Disappointment crashed onto him like the first waves of a typhoon when he saw that the statues were still standing. "You—you kept them?"

"Hm?" Kevin did not turn around. "What'd you say?"

It was obvious to the young man that his captor was sitting on the edge of two powerful emotions. A mental conversation fluctuated between logic and morality. Keeping the affinity and good favor of his crew while preserving the idea of being *the good guy*. His jaw clenched when they reached the spacious front yard.

Jekyll was curious about a spot a few feet away from his owner. His wet nose brushed through grass that was overdo to be mowed. Each property around them held a similar characteristic—some boasted wildflowers which brightened up the otherwise bleak and vapid neighborhood. Wyatt did not allow his dog to stray far. "There aren't any landmines or anything, right?"

"Wh—do you think we've gone batshit?"

"They sent you to steal my dog because they think it'll keep the infected away." When it was said out loud, the older man's cheeks dyed red. "Why are we just standing here?"

Kevin rubbed his forehead with his thumb and forefinger. A moment rolled by before he pursed his lips and exhaled a strident whistle that sliced the air. Jekyll's tail curls inwards.

"Nice." His lips curled. "Basically a codeword to get into the clubhouse."

"Oh, my God. Shut the fuck up." He spat, turned to face him, and dived in with, "I *could* have shot your ass!"

Wyatt understood this to be true and nodded once. In a matter of seconds, his expression transformed from being guarded to being bruised. Like waking from a lucid dream, his consciousness floated back into reality. Ahead of him was a boarded up Colonial-style home full of armed individuals who wanted nothing more than to strongarm Jekyll from him. His grip tightened on the leash.

Yet, there was no movement from inside the house or anywhere on the property. Kevin frowned and whistled again, louder and with more breath under it. Jekyll did not seem to be much of a fan of the noise and whimpered with eyes set to the man.

He looked at Wyatt. "Stay here."

"If I run, you'll know where to find me."

Kevin rolled his eyes and ventured a few steps into the lawn. Slow, deliberate steps, as if playing along that there were indeed landmines planted on the property, waiting to obliterate him with any improper step. Just as he began to purse his lips for another signal, the front door cracked open.

A tall woman with a full-face of makeup peeked out and nodded once in acknowledgement. Her eyes never left the dog.

Taking this as affirmation to continue forward, Kevin clicked his tongue in a quick couplet and gestured his new acquaintances to move up. Wyatt paused to ascertain the situation. There was a moment where he felt like he was in some obscure horror film. The sun's still out, he thought to himself. But it's still scary.

\-

The living room would have been considerably more inviting a few months prior to their meeting. As Wyatt remained seated on a rickety barstool with Jekyll at his feet, he looked around with quiet accomplishment. He was finally in the blue house and dared to ask a question to the room full of strange individuals who watched him as if he were the pilot of a new television show—with judgment, expectation.

"Why did… First, let me just say that the place looks *great*." No natural light came in, pardon the bands that struggled through boards attached to the windows. The refrigerator was unplugged and pressed against the back door to prevent entrance. Scented candles attacked his nose and highlighted the amount of dust that hung in the air. "So, um, why did you keep the gnomes?"

Kevin massaged the bridge of his nose as he leaned against a sealed closet to the right of Wyatt. Behind the young man was the front door, easily accessible if he felt comfortable or idiotic enough to attempt an escape. In front of him was a gaudy olive couch with three individuals sat upon it as if they claimed thrones in a royal court.

The woman with makeup flashed a smile before her heavy cheeks hung low; gravity itself was pushed with all of its strength. Loose, blonde-gray curls were planted high on her crown while the sides of her head were kept short. Her neck was not blended well. A visible line above her throat offered everyone in the room a timeline as to when she stopped caring. The blush on her cheeks reminded Wyatt of a Victorian-era baby dying of a fever.

Perhaps she always dressed this performative, he blinked. Or perhaps she finally feels comfortable enough now that societal expectations were of less importance.

Her voice was pleasant, though. A vague melody strung together each pre-meditated word. "You have received an offer from Kevin. However, as you are sitting in front of us with your canine companion still in-hand, we assume you have declined."

Embarrassment was the only word that could describe how Wyatt felt in the moment. Once more did he take in his surroundings and even searched for hidden cameras in desperation to help reconcile the absurd situation. "Um," he looked to her and the two men on either side of her. Through his breath, "That is correct. Sorry?"

Kevin peeled himself away from the wall and lifted his finger to stop the apparent council from further delegating amongst themselves. "He actually... My apologies. May I speak?" The Madame did not object. "He gave me a lot to think about in terms of how we *could* handle things."

"Think?" She tilted her head, then shook it with a disapproving smack of the lips. "You were sent to *do*, Kevin."

The man to her left wore a heavy sweater and his pale, sweaty face meant he was just as hot as Wyatt could imagine. "Not to be presumptuous, but, we are not here to engage conflict of any kind," he said while visibly ignoring a bead of sweat that was caught by his eyelash. "So, if the boy declined and brought us an alternative, I think we should at least hear him out."

"Thank you," Wyatt's captor bowed his head. The Madame was irritated, but knew that the job of a council was to be a shared voice instead of a singular, ruling authority. She returned the bow during a stuttered rolling of the eyes. "He claims that his home has clean water, a fair amount of food, and…" Kevin looked at the man who secretly sweltered inside of his wool sweater. "Air conditioning."

The Sweater adjusted his pair of round-framed glasses and felt renewed hope rise. "Food, you say?" A nonchalant play off. "Enough for this group, do you think?"

"How long would it last multiple-households for?" The Madame interjected. She leaned forward on her seat. Wyatt received a visual cue from Kevin that he was allowed, and obligated, to reply.

"Well," he started. "Long enough, I think."

"What does that mean?"

"I mean, I don't think that this whole thing is going to last for much longer. Another month, tops, if you were to ask me."

Another male voice piped up to the woman's right. It was tired and droned on with unenthusiastic vigor. "No way. Years, at least." The room became quiet. Someone in the group of onlookers that stood behind the couch scratched their eyebrow and looked away. "In order for those sleazeballs in the CDC to regulate an antidote, it's going to take years."

Wyatt pondered over this, as did those in the room who nodded and murmured to each other. He asked, "Can I ask, what do you think is the worst case scenario?"

The Unenthusiastic furrowed his brow and motioned to those surrounding him. "This. We're already living in the worst case scenario. We got the equivalent of four families here living off of canned green beans and applesauce. You see how long it takes for the government to respond to a crisis like a—a hurricane?" He sniffed. "It's gonna take years."

"I see your point, but don't you think you guys responded to the whole cat virus thing with, erm, a little *too much* haste?" The three on the couch became uncomfortable when questioned. "It doesn't have to be the end of the world. We just have to wait it out. Together, maybe. I'm sure there are still other people in the neighb—"

"No, no. They're all here," The Sweater claimed flatly. "There are a few children upstairs, there is a pregnant woman from East Corrado Street…" His voice trailed away when The Madame threw him a caustic glare. "The point being is, we are ready for whatever may come. Be it another wave, or, less-likely yet still likely, the quarantine never lifting."

Wyatt looked down to his Jekyll, who picked up on the gesture in his peripheral and reciprocated while heavily panting. "You live in constant fear that the infected are going to come back." They did not respond to him, so he made eye contact with the alleged council. "Even though I haven't even seen a single cat in weeks. The police, however you feel about them during all of this, are doing their job and they're doing it well enough that—"

"Please," The Madame raised her hand to silence him. A deep feeling of exhaustion settled behind her eyes. When he scouted the room, *everybody's* eyes reflected exhaustion. "Just give us your dog."

"No."

With a slow blink, The Unenthusiastic joined. "We're not asking you for your food or water. You can keep all of that. We know how to scavenge."

"Then scavenge another dog."

Wyatt's muscles were wound in tension. He still carried with him the pathetic knife, but he would not know how to navigate going about using it against a group of people. If one were to attack him, there could be enough time to defend himself, but would inevitably end up leaving his dog open for capture.

Jekyll had never been formally trained in any sort of defense or bitework, but he was naturally capable due to his mix of breeds. In such a hypothetical, he would wise up after a moment and retaliate, but any bite would be non-lethal. No one dog had enough momentum to fend off a group of—Wyatt counted in his head—*eight* people.

The Madame calmed the room who had become irritable. Another woman with straight brunette hair descended the stairs without making a noise. She kept her wooden eyes on the scene but remained unobtrusive.

With a strange flourish of her right hand, the woman caught in a perpetual blush licked her top lip with a slow drag and used this time to think of her next response. "Kevin," she did not look away from Wyatt. The bearded man straightened his spine like a meerkat keeping watch over his kingdom. "Give your gun to Jose."

With a pout that trickled away from his face as soon as he became cognizant of it, Kevin approached The Unenthusiastic and withdrew the pistol from his pocket.

The man, identified as Jose, inspected it with a professional gaze. "You've used it." His tone hovered between dismissive and humored. "Yet they're both… Right here." Kevin apologetically nodded. "But, you've brought the dog to us, so I suppose you kept your end of the bargain."

"Yes, sir."

Jose nodded for a moment, then reached into a neon pink fanny pack that was hidden by an oversized golf polo. "The master is yours." A brass bullet was retrieved. "You can go ahead and start moving in your stuff." It was loaded into the empty chamber which snapped shut via a strike from the man's meaty palms.

Wyatt & Gene : *Part Two*

As if puppeteered by auto-pilot, Kevin walked past the council and stopped just before the stairs. The brunette woman waiting on the final step expressed disapproval through her wilted lips. She mouthed, "Really?" Wyatt gathered she did not expect the bearded man to accomplish whatever task he was sent out to do.

Kevin sighed and maybe felt the same. He walked past her and stopped when their shoulders brushed. Rigid, he apologized under his breath before continuing to the second story to disappear from view.

Wyatt was starting to doubt—well, everything. Sweat dampened the leash in his left hand and felt a cold chill that should not have existed while in this sweltering house. "Okay, well," he blurted. "Is there room here for anybody else?"

The council was stunned. They looked at each other with the same expression shared between them: arched brows, mouths agape. The Sweater was the first to speak. "I'd like to argue that there is barely enough room for us. If you're looking to join our—"

"No, I'm not." His words were quick when a clear intention formed in his head. He backpedaled. "I'm asking if you would like to send people over with me." The thought of his roommate returning home to a house full of dirty strangers made him giddy, the prank of the century, but resolved to meditate on that imagery at a later time. "I have gas to spare, an unused bedroom, a comfortable couch."

The Madame exclaimed, "And you'll cleave your dog in two so both camps can share it. A wonderful idea!" Wyatt leaned back in the barstool and felt his equilibrium give away. He recovered, but it was not graceful. She continued after giggling. "We are not in the business of compromise.

"You must admit that you are at a great disadvantage. We know where you live, we know what you have, and we know that you are unarmed." Her legs crossed over one another in a slow, coquettish movement. It was obvious that she received a sort of sick thrill from her interim position of power.

Wyatt paused, then nodded without giving her the courtesy of eye contact. "So, you're willing to leave me alone as long as you have my dog." Two-out-of-three nodded. The Unenthusiastic was busy admiring his weapon. "And literally none of you in this house had a dog to bring over?"

The Madame smiled. "I'm allergic." A simple shrug. The idea of her skin breaking out did not bother her. She claimed that as long as the safety of her household was secured, she would gladly accept dipping into the antihistamine cache they kept on hand. "And the HOA had a breed restriction or disallowed pets outright. I've been curious as to how you've kept your dog under the radar for all this time."

"That's easy." He dropped his shoulders and swung his gaze to his best friend. He panted, just as unaware of his future as Wyatt was. "I didn't tell anyone."

Jekyll's features were branded in Wyatt's brain. He had spent many mornings parsing through the dog's fur with a comb made for his coarse fur. There was a discoloration along his neck that blended into a series of half-visible spots on his spine. His tail always drifted left when not in motion.

They knew nothing about him.

The council was cordial in that they allowed the young man to commit the dog's image to memory. Another draft found its way into the home and The Sweater spoke up. "You can come and see him," he decided for the three. "We don't want to cause any more unnecessary stress—not for either of you. We just…"

As his voice faded away, The Madame took the lead. "We are looking out for the good of all of us. You are but one life," she shook her head when a sudden sense of responsibility dawned on her. "And we are many."

Sweat formed on Wyatt's upper lip. "You don't even know if it's true." He wiped his mouth with the back of his hand and straightened his posture. "Keeping him here because dogs and cats don't get along. That's antiquated bullshit," his voice turned into a shout and The Unenthusiastic responded by raising his weapon. "You're all living in some deluded fantasy. It's *not that bad*, we are *not doomed.*"

Wyatt's forehead was fit between the iron sights of the revolver. His body convulsed with unkerned anxiety. The Unenthusiastic took in a deep breath and released it through speech. "Are you going to keep giving us trouble?"

He wanted so much to expel the first sardonic reply that came to mind. Yes, he compressed. I'm going to fucking kill you if you take my dog.

His mouth opened like the dawning of a new day. "No," Wyatt's tongue stretched. "I guess as long as I can… I can see him."

A pleasant hum from The Madame. "What is he called? We don't want to be rude and rename him."

"Hyde," he lied and felt his lower lip twitch. "Like—like *rawhide*."

The Sweater pushed up his glasses and smiled. "That's a good name." Wyatt creaked his neck to face the man and wore a deflated scowl. The air between them became stale. "Yes, well," he cleared his throat. "We will let you return home, but, just so you know, we don't have any food for him."

Wyatt blinked, widened his eyes, then fought an exasperated sigh. "Okay, so I should bring you all the food I have." This was not a question. He had no choice unless he wished to see his dog starve to death.

"And any toys," The Sweater raised his finger. "We have to keep Hyde-y occupied. Don't worry, we're going to be great to him."

-

Being lonely had never been a possibility until Wyatt tried to fall asleep that night. His feet were cold and they had not been cold in five years. The exact spot where Jekyll would curl up and snore was a vacuous crater. Any subtle ambiance supplied by his companion was gone.

The mid-night smacking of the lips, or a deep sigh whenever he inched closer up Wyatt's legs until he found a half-moon spot that was a perfect fit just under the man's butt.

He tried to focus on his breathing and pretended it was Jekyll's. Unsuccessful. He tried sleeping on his stomach for the first time since he was a kid and, again, it did not help. Why would it? It was uncomfortable and his pillow was too soft and the bed was too firm and his socks were still on and…

Images appeared of his dog whining from confusion as he was forced to leave the complex and obliged to return with a cardboard box of food and toys. The look on those people's faces, Wyatt squeezed his eyes with enough force that a firework display appeared for him. Like they're doing me a favor—doing *him* a favor.

The covers that trapped all of his body heat were thrown off in a frustrated toss and he felt the hard floor connect with his damp socks. He stared into the darkness that swallowed any details of his room. Wyatt's gaze staggered in multiple directions; double vision began to set in and obscure his sight even further. His steady breathing became thick with vibrato.

The same darkness extended to the streets outside of his home; the government decided to cut the power to most of the county in encouragement for families to evacuate into cities. It had been two months since his town was what the officials deemed as "overrun", though he would beg to differ. Armed forces came in fast and with precision. They swept each neighborhood with automatic weapons and cleared out any of the infected who did not already expire from a heart attack.

During the last month, their visits became sparse. He recalled an officer breaking into his home, as he did with his neighbors', and marched through the home with the intent to find any smuggled cats or kittens. Wyatt's property was in the clear, but he did hear intermittent gunshots from the adjacent yards.

There was a time when the streets were still busy with community even after the quarantine was imposed. Weeks went by and the houses in his neighborhood became derelict, one by one. He never knew where they went, but he imagined that when the families piled into their vehicles and headed to

Houston or Galveston. Wyatt held empathy for them, but did not agree with their actions.

He never once felt the desire to leave his small town. His truck had been idle for a week. The last time it was used was to scout for any grocery stores that were still open. Most were boarded up, but a one select grocer was used as bases for munitions some distance away. They were guarded by the police and rations of food were handed off by the box full. When asked, he said he had a wife and newborn daughter waiting for him back home.

Formula sat unused in his pantry, but the jars of baby food he was given in advance had a better flavor than he would have thought.

Wyatt had food, gasoline, and water. He should be grateful. There was no way for him to know how many people had died or were currently starving.

Even without a dog, he *should* be grateful.

The young man walked the same route that he would usually take with Jekyll and found it easier to clear the distance without a dog laboring by his side. Strung with anxiety, he extended his route but was careful to avoid the gnome house. This initiative took him into the adjacent neighborhood of Windham Court. The splay of woods he usually frequented was separated by a small canal—it could easily be jumped over without much effort. He had thought about it several times before, though the obligation of walking his dog was usually the only exercise he allowed himself. Any desire to return to interesting spots never manifested into action.

The nearby houses were as large as the blue house that stained the back of his eyelids. Multiple stories, too-many windows, porches, patios, pools. He wondered how many of them once contained dogs and how many had been abandoned and left to rot.

Wyatt considered this a scenic route as he had never encountered the slick, recently repaved street. Connecting roads in his neighborhood were ridden with potholes and bleached from the sun—the variable plants including aloe were charred, close to death. Even the trees in Windham were healthier. The amount of new imagery helped to temporarily ease the suffering that stabbed at his heart every time his thoughts faltered.

Behind a stretch of houses was a divot in the ground and a wall of trees perched on the incline. Figuring that no one would stop him, he crouched and cleared someone's yard until he found himself searching for footing as he descended the slope. The clean denim jeans he wore were certain to be stained with grass and soil, but it did not bother him.

His shoes stuck to thick mud that collected in the slender reservoir and occasionally snagged on breached roots. Once oriented, Wyatt looked up and around. A thick canopy was divided by a thin chasm acting as a window to the night sky.

There were more stars than usual. Constellations that were once subdued and lost to light pollution stuck their heads out like a family of timid rabbits.

There was protection from every angle. He could stay here and die and no one would know. Hidden from view and intent on keeping his mind occupied, Wyatt trudged along the bank while ignoring the wet, soft mud leaking through his shoes.

With unwavering commitment, the young man kept silence close to him. If anybody were still in these homes, they might be cozied up inside with a gun—or multiple. The wrong move or sound could mean the end of his life. Branches and roots snagged on his clothes and pulled him back like the hands of hell themselves were trying to prevent him from gaining access to heaven.

Wyatt reached the end of the line. The inflow chamber, barricaded by evenly spaced iron bars, sang a haunting tune as he stared into the maw. What sounded like laughter from a pixie drew him nearer. He patted his right pocket for the cell phone he was grateful to have brought along. Low-battery did not prevent the built-in flashlight from beaming with full force. A collection of eyes met with him within the damp tunnel.

-

A stretchy garbage bag was hauled into the largest room of the blue house by the bearded man whose face reflected regret. He lived in a swirling pit of potentiality. Voices from downstairs coo and jeer at their new companion. Sometimes, a bark ripped through the house and met Kevin's ears. Even when he closed the door, the dog, who had been nicknamed Hyde, exhaled whines loud enough to push through several walls and disrupt any attempt at sleep.

This master bedroom was desirable—and he had to keep reminding himself of that. Whoever accomplished the most for the house gained respite in the form of privacy. As an added reward, a memory foam mattress wrapped around his spine and kept his body still. When he shut his eyes, he could imagine himself floating above the Earth.

Next to him was his wife, the straight-haired woman who was so wired she could not even fathom closing her eyes. Even in her peripheral vision, she kept a close watch on him. Kevin could feel her eyes stain his left cheek. "Nellie?"

She sucked in her lower lip. "Yeah." A high-pitched whir in her ear appeared and dimmed within seconds. An old story her mother once told her fluttered into her consciousness: *When your ears ring, an angel is speaking to you.*

With exhaustion, he asked, "What's going on?"

"You…" Penelope turned to face him. She did well to hide her comfort. "You doomed that poor dog. These people don't know how to take care of something like that. They can barely take care of themselves. The other day, we were fighting about a *tea bag*, Kevin—of all things, a…"

The woman hissed and clenched either fist. She wanted to punch the bed but suppressed her tantrum. Her hands instead found their way to cup a bulge under her shirt. "I get why you did it."

Kevin did not open his eyes and felt his posture shrink inwards—the feeling of a vacuum pulling all of his muscles into a fine point located in the center of his gut. "For us, the baby."

"And what happens when someone else does something that *pleases the council*?" The latter half of her sentence was dripping in so much sarcasm, she seemed to adopt a brand new persona. A voice he had never heard before. "They kick us out and we're back to snuggling tight in the hallway."

"It's not gonna happen." A sigh escaped his lungs like a gentle breeze from a fan. "I'm just going to have to keep sucking up. Kissing ass."

"Sucking dick, you mean?" She raised her eyebrows and he snapped his eyes open. "If that's what it's gonna take, right, we just do whatever they want us to do because they have a gun?" Kevin tilted his head to her and hesitated to respond. The tired woman felt her eyes dry out. "Don't be mad at me because I'm right."

He leaned forward and stretched his arms over his head until he heard a pop come from either shoulder. The man decompressed into a slump. His posture had always been bad and now, maybe, he had the chance to fix it. Kevin's fingers squeezed the strange foam.

"Listen," he started and combed the balding spot on the top of his head. "That kid from earlier, he gave me a lot to think about. He asked me—he said that he doesn't think that this whole scenario is going to last too much longer. I don't know why but I think I agree with him."

Penelope pulled covers up from her feet. She did not feel the need to reply. With a slow drag, he continued, "But these people think it's going to last forever and who knows how insane they're going to become because of it."

"Are you kidding? You're the one who wanted to do this. Now you're worried—look, they're already driven to lunacy." She rolled her eyes and burrowed under the comforter. "They act like they're world leaders meeting in Genova." He became swallowed by a new realm of thoughts, more potentials. Penelope noticed this, cleared her throat, and gently whispered his name. "I don't mean to blame you. What are you thinking?"

"Oh," a sigh rattled. "Thinking about Wyatt's house, how he has an extra room and a bunch of supplies."

"That's his name? That kid? Well," she lowered the lush blanket from her mouth. "What do you want to do? Does he also have a memory foam bed or was it really that important to you in the first place?"

Kevin scratched at his forehead until a red mark appeared. He looked to the window to his right, expecting to receive insight from the moon but instead stared at plywood boarded into the frame.

"I mean, they already have the dog," she said. "And it would only help them to have more resources. No one's going to complain about having food to eat."

"Right? I was seriously just thinking about that." There was a rekindled spark to his tone. It tapered off when he asked her, "But, how do you feel about this end-of-the-world scenario? How long do you honestly think it's going to last?"

Penelope sucked on her lips and two lumps rose from under the blanket. A hidden shrug. "You just gotta promise me one thing. Kevin, you have to promise—"

"The dog," he threw his head back and collapsed back onto the bed. "I know." Tight with exhaustion, his fingers expanded a few times to stretch his palms. They eventually ended up clutching his face in a brace. "We'll figure it out."

A wilting pause from Penelope. "Because it's not fair—"

"Yeah," Kevin cut her off with a sharp motion of his left hand. "I know. I'm an asshole. We will figure it out."

The woman's eyes kept on her husband until her head began to shake at the sight of him. A coward hid under a bushy beard. She could imagine his face overgrown with the bristly mess just so he can avoid being seen by the world. Penelope sniffed and made herself comfortable.

He was trusted enough by the council to break into someone's home with the only gun they shared between them. If he had lost it or was killed, all of the leverage garnered by the small community would be rendered into dust. The weight that must have fallen onto his shoulders, the woman considered. It would have been more than I can handle.

"Hey, Kev," Penelope forced out. He shifted but did not respond. Her throat felt like it was beaming a bright red light. "You, erm, did a—a good job by not killing him. The boy. Wyatt."

He weighed his response before twisting his mouth into a cute smile. "I mean, I thought so." She rolled her eyes and turned away from him with an audible groan. This did not bother him. The compliment was enough.

Wyatt & Gene : *Part Three*

Wyatt threw open the door to his home with sweat and filth caked to his skin. Plant matter collected under his fingernails and he had managed to tear a chunk of flesh from his right ring finger. He cradled the hand under his damp armpit. The wound, stinging but insignificant, did not matter. He could clean it, sanitize it, and wrap it with gauze in the span of a few minutes.

Each thrum of his heartbeat that sounded in his ear mimicked the ticking of an unseen clock.

After bandaging himself, the man rifled through his cabinets with the occasional wince. All of the reserves he had collected were carelessly tossed on the ground. Cans of beans, boxes of animal crackers. A palpitation rippled through his chest when he located a can of tuna.

He thought he had acquired multiple over the course of the last two months—at least one more. There was another minute spent combing through the shelves before giving up with an audible sigh. One was enough, he hoped.

Finding a can opener was his next task. A short period of catching his breath was adopted as a necessary bullet point in his plan. The remainder of a half-empty water bottle was tossed down his gullet and the hard swallow ached his lungs. The crinkling of the material was loud in his empty home.

Wyatt found himself back in the streets and on his way to the retention pond with a tote bag looped around his neck. The paring knife used as a flimsy negotiation tool the day before had been tucked through a belt loop.

He devoted more attention to silence during his short trip. Loose leaves and small puddles were avoided in their entirety. The man considered the tight-fitting work boots strapped to his feet much too loud as it was.

When Wyatt breached the neighborhood full of expensive homes, he resolved to slink behind any available foliage to ensure his surreptitious stalking continued unnoticed. While scaling the divot, the weak blade pricked his skin and bled through the jeans he already decided to throw away after this nightmare scenario was completed. The sticky mud was easier to navigate upon his return.

Only a few feet from the inlet, he crouched and dropped the tote to the ground. A rusted can opener could barely penetrate the sealed tuna but a good shimmy-or-two later was enough to separate the lid. He used his fingers to do the rest of the work. To his surprise, he did not injure himself any further.

His back gained a sharp ache when he strafed over a puddle and placed the can between the bars. Wyatt was cautious and kept his breaths as silent as possible. His fingers dug into the wet meat and flicked a clump into the darkness.

The man could hear the calls of kittens—he was not insane, his tired mind did not manufacture these apparitions. There was no reason to flash the light from his cell phone again, it only upset them the last time. It was dangerous for the creatures to be vocal.

Wyatt closed his eyes and tuned into the expansive chamber before him. He could hear gentle mewing accompanied by the sound of moisture failing and reverberating throughout. There was no way for him to squeeze through. His arm could swing around in the darkness and hope to fetch one, but he could be scratched in the process.

There was no way for him to know which cats were infected, but he figured the water they scavenged would be carrying the virus.

That was the overwhelming theory, at least.

One call was louder than the others. He opened his eyes and felt his heart sink. A kitten had gathered enough courage to let itself be known. Brown-faced, dull eyes, and a pouting expression. The way it limped forward unnerved the young man. Curiosity blemished its eyes—about the stranger who could offer sustenance, about what was beyond the damp home they had made.

Wyatt forced down a swallow and readied the tote bag.

-

A long exhale was followed by a short and soft gasp. Behind Kevin's eyes rested a hundred pounds of pressure. He held onto lucidity by tossing to lay on his side whenever he felt himself drifting.

One minute, the sound of an airy and mental voice commanded. Then you have to get up. Get up, get up—*you piece of shit, get out of bed.*

He lurched his body to the left and marveled at how incredible the mattress felt under him. In all of his forty-something years, he had never received a night of sleep so glorious and healing. All of the small aches in his body no longer existed. Why would they? It was as if the memory foam took a knife to his pain and slit its throat. A ceremonial bloodletting to welcome in a new era of a younger, more revitalized Kevin.

Gotta drain my savings and get me one of these, he thought as he ran his fingers through what was left of his oily, curly hair. He checked on Penelope, who could not help but let intermittent snores fly free. The man smiled and felt pin-pricks from his unkempt beard.

There was an attempt to peek through the tight cracks between the pieces of plywood that barricaded the windows. Only a little light, probably just from the moon. His hands began to quake when he thought of the series of events he promised himself would unfold.

Penelope's voice cracked, "Hey." He turned to her and returned the greeting. She invited him to sit next to her. With a weak smile, Kevin lowered himself and leaned in to kiss her. She responded with a lethargic peck. "You gonna do it?"

"I have to. Right?" He wanted her to convince him otherwise.

"Right," the woman said. "In and out. Just"—she yawned—"don't get caught. I'll get up in a little."

He rolled his eyes and stifled a laugh. "Yep. Yup." Kevin lifted himself from the bed, stretched his back out as a form of procrastination, then made his way to their door. His hand hovered over the metallic knob. "If his door's locked, I'll just be outside."

There was a moment where Penelope wanted to argue, but the mattress was calling her name. She sighed and her nostrils twitched. With this, her husband bid her good-night and exited the room. The woman stayed upright, balanced with both hands, and waited for Mr. Sandman to kiss her on the forehead.

Kevin, the embodiment of caution, finally felt the weight of his plan. His whole life had been spent rejecting risks and following the path he could see with his own two eyes. It was unfortunate that, as he clumsily moved down the stairs, the only thing in front of him was darkness.

He applied pressure to each step with his big toe and waited to hear a squeak, creak, voice, or shout. By the time he felt the hardwood floor under his feet, Kevin had lost a majority of his energy. The man wanted to sprint back upstairs and throw himself onto the comfortable bed with his wife, to return to the room that he earned and deserved. Why was it his responsibility to bring back the mutt to its owner?

Kevin managed to pick up a sour scent on his breath after a silent exhale. If he were to live with Wyatt, there could be a spare toothbrush. If not, he was sure that the roommate would not mind the occasional use as long as the brush was boiled after. By the time the quarantine lifted, he could just run to All-Mart and get him another.

The small promises of an improved quality of life—that is why he wished to return the dog. Moreover, this is why he felt like he *needed* to.

Once his eyes adjusted, he searched the floor. No sign of the creature. He stepped over someone's feet that stuck out from under a table before he entered the kitchen. With the cold tile and drafty open space, Kevin should have known that someone would decide to sleep in front of the fridge.

An empty bottle of wine was on its side and rested against the individual's cheek. He knew the name of the man as Roger, someone he had never liked particularly well and someone who was generally disliked throughout the encampment. In the drawers to his left should have been sheathed knives. There was a possibility that any item with the possibility of being a weapon was confiscated, but, since he had no way to be sure, he continued with the image of his future deep in his mind's eye.

The sound of his calloused heel scraping against the tile stirred Roger from his shallow slumber. He perched himself against the fridge and smacked his dry lips. "Hey, man," his voice was chalky. The drunk man looked around the kitchen and blinked to see through the darkness. "Is it late?"

Kevin did not respond with words, but instead a slow and gangly jig. He rocked his arms side-to-side and pretended he wore a hat, which he then tipped to the still-intoxicated man. Roger watched on as there was little else he could do. With every blink, his eyes became heavier. Soon, gentle snoring resumed.

A weird dream to forget the next morning.

With his heart beating triple-time, he was winded but proud of his successful ploy. He pillaged two-out-of-three drawers and found nothing sharp or dangerous. A spoon, maybe, if he could rip off the end and use it as a shank.

He shook his head. There was no part of him that wanted to maim someone else, especially someone while they were sleeping. No one in this house deserved to die. They were all looking out for each other.

However, the attitude of Jose had become frightening over the last few weeks. He held onto the only gun and all of its ammunition. That dumb fanny pack, Kevin licked the top row of his teeth. A spoon will have to do.

-

Inside the claustrophobic hiding space of a strange man's closet, Jekyll curled into a ball and tucked his nose under his paw. His eyes remained in fear that, once closed, everything would end.

Two different voices snore. Phlegmy and stuttered. Unfamiliar.

He knew Wyatt's sounds—the occasional cough in the middle of the night, or a yawn before he stumbled to the bathroom. Slow, steady, and clean breathing.

The dog knew to keep quiet as he had already been screamed at for whining all throughout the evening. A large man with a droll voice lifted his fist and threatened to attack him, but was stopped by another man wearing an oversized sweater. Jekyll did not understand the words exchanged but was grateful. If he could find a way to thank The Sweater, he would.

In this makeshift home was the smell of stagnant air and mildew. Heat surrounded the dog and tried to bite its way through his coarse fur. He wanted to pant, to cool down, but was afraid of stirring the scary man who did not have someone to stop him from initiating another attack. The room was dark and the closet made it darker, so how could Wyatt ever find him? Should he bark and risk the abuse?

A rattle of the doorknob and he lifted his head. Jekyll waited for another sound of equal-or-greater hope. The sound of metal-scraping-metal perked his ears.

The door opened with such caution that the dog wondered if it were just the wind. A familiar head peeked in. The man who confronted him and Wyatt earlier. Jekyll ducked his head and kept watch.

In his right hand was some sort of tool he must have used to open the door. Jekyll could not get a good view as Kevin disappeared after just a moment of return. The closet door blocked the dog's line of sight, but he kept his senses tuned into the man who kept himself quiet.

Something rustled. The sound of jingling and then a tight sigh. No movement for a while, and then the flat sound of footsteps against the carpet as Kevin receded to the door. Jekyll lifted himself from the seated position, unfurling himself and bumping the inside of the closet. The man ducked, his eyes wide, and made direct eye contact with him.

A husky voice drifted in and out, "Sit down." It lost all strength by the second syllable. Kevin's breathing became louder as he beckoned the animal forth. Little, almost imperceptible clicks of the tongue dropped out of his mouth and found their way to Jekyll. The dog slinked from his hiding spot, his tail low and pressed against his bottom, but wagging regardless.

-

Kevin switched his attention from the dog to the two in the bed. He had never been allowed in Jose's room before and was surprised to see that The Madame also cozied up in a similar memory foam bed to his. If he wished to be daring, he could finally see who she was under the mask of makeup. Not now, he corrected himself. Maybe not ever.

He pushed on the dog's hind to expedite him out of the room. Sounds of rustling and scuffing should have woken up the two, but if the blubbering snores from Jose were not enough to wake up The Madame, nothing would.

Jekyll's nails dragged against the carpet until they scraped against the wooden floor that belonged to the hallway. Kevin tried to hush the animal but his deep panting was intertwined with a hoarse whine. His tail wagged—impulsive and stressed—and as they reached the staircase, the man felt his heart launch out of his chest.

The dog rushed down each step, each bounce as loud as the last, and broke into the living room like the sound of a thousand screws tossed down the stairs. Those who were asleep on the couch or the floor woke from their slumber and hissed for the creature to be quiet. A woman groaned, cursed, and swiped at Jekyll when his nose rubbed against her hanging hand. Kevin stayed low and stuck to the corners of the room. His end goal was to reach the front door.

Once he could open it, the bearded man knew that the dog would run back to his home and, hopefully, everyone in the room would be much too disoriented to comprehend the situation and he would have the chance to follow suit.

Jekyll jumped against the door with his heavy paws and vomited a sharp bark. Each voice that belonged to those in the living room acted as a piece of a puzzle. Everyone raised to their feet and began investigating the cause of their aggravation.

A soft, yellow beam from a dying flashlight cascaded into the living room like the floodlights of a prison in search of a renegade convict. Kevin moved along the far left wall and felt a pair of hands grip his shoulders. He was spun on his heels to face the stairs. Jose's tired voice spoke through a yawn.

"You're taking my dog?" This threw the room into a frenzy. One woman claimed that everyone held custody of the animal while an older man, who had decided to rename him Franklin, called out the name and patted his knees with no response from Jekyll. "This whole thing was *my* idea," Jose said, irritated enough to raise his voice. "My idea, my dog! Don't be selfish!"

The individual that held onto Kevin was distracted, evidenced by him shouting ideas for a potential schedule in which everyone could take turns. "George on Tuesdays, Beth, then Reggie…"

Beth's voice cut through the noise, "There are eight of us!"

"Michelle is allergic, she don't want the dog. Also, Kevin and Penelope—"

The bearded man took advantage of the moment by stomping his right foot onto the respective toes of his captor. A holler, and then a slick punch to the chin.

Kevin stepped over the fallen body and slipped through another pair of hands as he reached towards the front door. He managed to unlock the sliding mechanism when Jose called his name. Jekyll did not stop scratching at the door. Another woman was approaching the dog while slinking to him in a slow crouch.

"Never thought it'd be you, bud." A wincing Jose trained his pistol to the rogue.

A dull click.

When he checked the empty cylinder, he expressed a confused grunt.

The woman lurched forward to snatch Jekyll but received a harsh reality check when the door flung open and forced her glasses into the bridge of her nose. She gasped and collapsed to the floor. With the broken nose suffocating her with fresh blood, her hands moved away from the dog to apply pressure.

Kevin whispered an apology and squeezed through the small crack he had made. When the door closed behind him, the cacophony of voices became less terrifying.

Those who still resided in that silly house cast blame unto each other. Jose's voice was the most distinct until a flagrant howling from The Madame bested those who dared to speak alongside her. He was a few feet away from the doorstep, his eyes searching the ground for Jekyll, when he heard her shout, "That pregnant *bitch* is gone, too!"

His heart swelled with relief before panging with fear. Kevin's focus shifted from locating the dog to finding his wife. He picked up his pace and rounded to the side of the blue house.

Penelope waited on the first story roof. A slim plateau allowed her enough room to hide from anyone who thought to look out of the window. On the ground below them were two suitcases that spilled open upon a previous impact. Kevin inspected what she bothered to take with her. Three of his outfits, three of hers. The most comfortable clothing that either of them owned.

She waved at him and whispered, "What do I do now?"

"You have to just—just jump."

"Are you going to catch me?!"

"What?" He shook his head. "No! Just—please! Jump!"

The drop was high enough for her to roll her ankle. He petered his temper by forcing himself to soothe her. "It's okay," Kevin said while lifting her. Penelope grabbed at their items and he told her that he would gather them later. "You remember the address? Do you—okay, it's eleven-thirty-one Oregon. Right down—"

A horrible voice rang—a ceramic hammer shattering against a brass bell. "*Kevin!*" He almost let go of his wife at the sight of The Madame. With frizzed hair and a hastily applied face of makeup, she looked cartoonish and absolutely manic. The woman gripped either end of a child's softball bat before sliding each hand to grasp the handle.

Penelope hobbled away when her husband whispered a reassuring phrase to her. She found respite against the corner of a wall and the beginning of a fence. The sensation of cold metal against his right hip supplied him with enough confidence to approach the woman with a held breath.

"We gave you a *good* room!" She swung downwards, not even close to the man's body. "We gave that bitch *tuna*"—another swing—"and *chocolate!*" This time, The

Madame managed to clip Kevin's left knee. The pain was uncomfortable but not enough to stop his retaliation.

When she reeled the bat over her head and handed over complete vulnerability, her arms loosened just as Kevin flourished the shiv from his waistline. Penelope yelped, "Kevin! Stop!" His teeth gritted and he resolved to hold the weapon to her throat instead of piercing the flesh.

The Madame gulped. A bulge traveled down her neck and ebbed under the blade. Her eyes were not on him. "What? What are you doing?" Kevin pressed the metal further into her skin. It was not sharp enough to cause any damage this way. "What are you looking at?"

Despite being held up by the enraged man, The Madame spoke towards a new direction. "What is that? What—what's in your hand?" Her voice was as gentle as possible. Kevin frowned and felt his grip weaken. He spotted movement in his peripheral and pulled away to take in a better view.

~*~

A drab room integrates many colors from a monochromatic spectrum of brown. On top of an antiquated desk, something that would be better off in the storage unit of a collector than a therapist's office, is a lamp with a frosted glass shade. It softens the room even more and helps create a sleepy atmosphere. The couch on which Kevin sat is too soft for his liking. Its material is like sticky flesh as it sticks to his skin with every movement.

He leans forward and the slick material squelches under his weight. Either hand is kept folded under his chin as he stares at Dr. Gene Belmont and waits for the completion of an obnoxious, slow-paced scribbling by hand. The therapist inhales through his nostrils and returns his attention to the client without blinking. "A bag full of cats?"

"Yep."

"You're hesitant to continue. Did something happen? What happened to Michelle?"

Kevin scratches behind his left ear. "She's fine. When we figured out what was going on, we…"

"How did you figure out what was going on?"

"I mean," the man's voice stiffens. "There was, I guess, wriggling in the bag and the sound of, like, *meowing*." Gene acknowledges the statement with a nod and stays quiet. "When we figured out what he had in there, we all kind of just shifted gears. You know, all the drama going on didn't matter."

"I could see why. The threat of infection would sober up anyone."

Kevin raises his eyebrows and leans back. "Yeah, right. So, after that… Oh, I don't know what to talk about next." This moment of introspection is not interrupted by Gene even though Kevin expects to hear his voice chime in at any moment. "I told him that I set his dog free and that changed the look in his eyes.

He was so ready to just—ah, fuck if I know what he was gonna do."

Dr. Belmont taps the side of his pen twice with his pointer finger. His long fingernails had always made these sessions uncomfortable. "Well, Kevin, he was ready to let the cat out of the bag." Kevin rubs his eyes with the palms of his hands. There was no smile or effort of emotion from the gentleman who wore a navy bow tie and checkered shirt. "In all seriousness, let's unpack this, step-by-step.

"He was upset with the camp for negotiating possession of his pet. That is understandable. He wished everyone in the house harm, even after being told there was a pregnant woman and children—"

"There were no children," Kevin shakes his head. "None. It was a part of the speech we prepared to make us seem needier than we actually were."

"Okay," Gene says. "But, he still *thought* that there were children and was ready to send them all to their death. How does that change your opinion of him?"

"It—I mean, it doesn't. I get it, I understand. If they stole my wife, I would be…"

"And he knew that he was putting his own pet's safety at risk in the process. Do we know if he had a plan beyond that? No, we don't, but we can assume he had a rescue plan for Hyde and while the lives of nobody else mattered to him, Wyatt would rather see-through with revenge than retribution. Keep in mind, he spoke of unity and peace at one point and even invited others into his own home."

Kevin chews on this information as if it were a piece of stale gum given to him from the pocket of a stranger. The man continues with, "At the start of our session, you told me that he had died. How did that happen?"

"Yeah," an ache grows in his stomach. "He let his guard down. Those cats."

"Oh." A healthy pause of consideration from both men. "So, he became infected?"

"Yeah. Yep. I think before everything happened, though."

"Were you the one to put him down?"

"I had ammunition," he starts with several bobs of his head, then a shrug. "But, no gun. Michelle ran away and we thought she abandoned us—Nellie and I, but she came out with Jose and… You know, we had permission from Wyatt. He had this look on his face when it happened like, 'Oh, well'."

Gene checks the time on a digital clock pinned to the wall. His eyes become distant. Kevin waits for a response until he feels he must clear his throat to capture the therapist's focus. There is an apology. "I am thinking of the infection. I had someone very close to me go through the symptoms. You said that Wyatt gave you permission?"

This admission should have made Kevin feel sorrow or empathy, but instead irritated him. With such limited time, why would… The man blinks and straightens his posture. "Yeah, he told me to take care of Jekyll and—yeah, not Hyde. I know what I said earlier, I just always thought it was Hyde."

"I see. Did you and Penelope take Jekyll in, then?"

His voice strains out, "For, like, a month, but neither of us even like dogs and we didn't really know how to take care of him. The quarantine lifted after Wyatt got Cat Scratch Fever. Good timing, I don't know how much longer Nellie and I could deal with the dog crying."

Gene clears his throat and a smirk cracks the edge of his mouth like a yawn destroying a dried clay mask. "'Cat Scratch Fever'?"

Kevin hisses a sad laugh. "Yeah, it's what a lot of people on the Internet are calling it now. Trying to make light of it, I guess."

"Speaking of, what happened to the cats that Wyatt brought?"

"Oh," a red flush. "We had to… You know, we had to do what we had to do."

He inhales through tight sinuses. "Have you flirted with the idea that Wyatt did not inherit the infection?"

"Is that a joke? How is that supposed to help me?" Kevin throws his hands up and Gene attempts to calm him down by reminding him of deep breathing exercises they had practiced twice before. When he sits, a sense of shame towards his regression needs to pass. After a minute of meditation, "Sorry. Yeah, no, of course. I wish I could have just sat there and watched him for a while, but everything happened so fucking fast. It makes my head spin."

"You did the best that anyone could do at that moment. No one was prepared for any of it, Kevin. You could have killed Wyatt when sent to his home but instead found a peaceful way to negotiate a tense situation. His actions were his own. His fate, as well."

A sigh, a pause, a lamenting moan. "I know, but…"

"Let me ask you this. Did, at any point, you have an opportunity to prevent Wyatt from the infection?"

Kevin thought about this for longer than felt comfortable. "If I didn't go to his house to begin with."

"If you didn't go to his house, he would have been shot dead by whomever else would have been sent with the gun."

"Jesus," he scoffs and leans back into the couch. The cushion absorbs him and he pulls away after finding additional hate for the cursed piece of furniture. "It's like saying his fate was sealed no matter what happened." Neither man speaks for a while. Kevin's brow collapses under the weight of an unspoken thought.

Gene bats his eyelashes and refers to the clock with the point of his pen. "Looks like we went over our time again." The man, heavy in stature, lifts himself from a wooden chair with a complex wicker backing. He moves to the door and opens it up while smiling with his eyes. His client is not able to bring energy to his feet or to his legs.

The therapist pokes his head out of the threshold and into the office. He lifts his pointer finger and assures someone seated in the lobby that he will be with them in a moment. "Kevin?" Gene turns back to the man and juts his head forward, a display of impatience. "No homework for this week. You're good to go."

Cade & Tawny

Sunday, 15th

I was told that writing down my thoughts would help me process them easier. Sounds good, but it took me fifteen minutes to write that first sentence. Not as long for the last one, and even less time for this one. Maybe I see where they are coming from.

Pardon me if I come off as the Patron Saint of Cheese, but, there is something about falling in love for real for the first time that eviscerates any chance of going back. Imagine traversing a jungle—the kind with blocky pyramids and overgrowth and snakes. You come across a rickety bridge constructed of rope and reclaimed wood. Somewhere along the way, someone thought it was a good idea to build the bridge and somewhere along the way, someone knew it was a good idea to leave it be.

You wish you knew who built the bridge or if it had simply just always been there. Someone designed it with those specific materials in mind and, even though it may not be the most efficient way to build a bridge, it got you across the gaping chasm filled with monsters that will eat you without hesitation.

The planks were once worn but are now covered in algaeic slime. If you, an untrained individual with low upper-body strength and the balance of an uneven chair, wish to cross the bridge, then you have to be aware of a very real chance that you will slip or the wood will splinter from under you. Those monsters are waiting.

It hurts to say that I've had children with someone that I did not love in the same way Tawny and I loved each other. It hurts to say that, against all odds, Carol is my support system once again. It hurts to remember the plot I chose for her. It hurts to never know if I did a good job.

Was there enough shade? Did she like her neighbors? Did the technician do a good enough job putting her back together? Worse yet, did she even like the outfit I chose for her?

Tuesday, 17th

I have to admit that there is no way I could have predicted the catharsis I'd feel after writing last night. My sleep was still anxious, but a different brand. Things that I've been wanting to tell my family, my children. Hopefully, in time, I will gather enough courage to hand these notes to them.

(eraser marks, unintelligible) have my grief stripped from me in the wake of other events. The world was mourning on their own time but I was—and according to Denver, still am—trapped in my own bubble. It's filling with hot carbon monoxide and I am quickly losing my breath.

Maybe I don't feel like writing as much today.

Friday, 20th

I have been blessed with five children. Two from Tawny's first marriage, one from mine, and two conceived of our own volition. We loved them all in equal measure and never could have known that we would create such a veritable troupe of comedians, artists, and philanthropists. Her eldest daughter died with her, but I always knew she would be a teacher. The kindness in Rhea's face, how her cheeks strengthened with every smile that forced her eyes into fine slits. That mess of hair and the striped cardigan that never left her body.

In a way, her death has taught me more than most of my professors have.

Her siblings still talk about her as if she is in the room with her. I really hate to say it, but she is not. She passed into that white light as soon as the car crumbled. It may help or hurt my children to know that, even while Rhea is no longer a part of this realm and is off exploring the potentials for her next incarnation, her mother is the one who stayed.

Saturday, 21st

Denver called me and put me on the phone with young Caden. He can form sentences now. It destroys me to witness a child grow and evolve in the way many others have not, in the way Tawny never had the chance to. I look at myself in the mirror and I want to vomit into my hands and smear it over the glass and pretend I am simply just a smudge and not a greying human being with lines and dark circles and yellow teeth and wispy hair.

I know that if the same infliction of aging took its unrelenting hold over a still alive Tawny, I would be sure to never look away. I would spend hours diving into those ridges in her cheeks, the smile lines on her forehead. Instead, she sits here on my bed and is only visible whenever I do not pay attention to her. Even in my peripheral vision, she has a head of thick brown hair with the curls that were inherited by Rhea and Bobby.

Right now, her mouth is moving but I don't know if she is speaking or singing. She is smiling, her teeth as perfect as they had been when she flew through the console. Maybe it is enough for her to be by my side. I don't need to hear her since I don't think I ever did.

Tuesday, 24th

How long have I been able to ignore Tawny's presence and still be able to function?

Since I started journaling at the request of my psychotherapist, she is becoming more visceral. Her body (eraser marks, unintelligible) reach out and feel her skin. Will it feel cold, or moist, or scaly? Will it feel like liquid nitrogen against my bare flesh?

For the love of God. It used to be so simple to be with her. I felt an honor, maybe a debt, like I was chosen. My thoughts aren't coming out right. She is stalking the room, speaking to me with some gesticulation that is too familiar. The way she swings her hips as she completes one pace. I wish I understood her. I can't even lipread, because the longer I look at her, the more blurry she becomes.

Steel wool is scraping the surface of my brain trying to understand what is happening. It should be becoming less real over time. It's been ten years and now she talks to me with more vigor and passion than even while she was alive.

Does she speak of the answers to the universe? Is she warning me of things to come? Is she inviting me to join her?

Wednesday, 25th

(pen scratches)

Friday, 27th

I rescheduled my appointment with Quang. If I show up looking like this, I'd have to tell him everything. Oh, God, I can feel myself grow older by the second. The longer I stay in this house, in my room, the more my skin becomes brittle and my bones feel dry and porous.

Wednesday, 1st

Bobby came to visit, which is very nice of him since I know how busy he is. He said that he and his partner are trying to adopt and my heart has never felt so full in my whole life. Yes, of course, I also love young Caden… But, I have a specific bias since I was not asked if I was okay with the name. I wasn't, but now it is less of a concern.

I have never met his partner Darren or Daryl, I can't remember. They have been together for three years. I understand why he would not want to bring him around. To a normal human with normal human eyes and a normal human brain, I can come across as quite mad. I've not a bigoted bone in my body—my children are darker than I am!

I am hoping that he thinks that I am insane and not homophobic or racist. It would break my heart if I had ever done something, said something of the like. I would rather be considered insane!

That being said, the Risperdal makes me feel like I can breathe. I was told I would not feel the effects for two weeks. Well, if that's the case, then I must be very sensitive to it. I am in the mood to write something else, but not here.

Friday, 3rd

Good and bad news! Good news, I am much more in tune with my body than I thought! The bad news, I am very sensitive to Risperdal and was discontinued treatment due to aggressive muscle spasms. We are considering Seroquel.

Overall, my session was fine. We may have spent more time talking about medicine and chemistry than any of my mental issues. Quang ended on a high note and asked if I had seen Tawny. I told him yes, but she is less vivid. Yesterday I hardly saw her at all.

He asked how I felt about it—classic therapist move. I wanted to tell him that I am afraid of losing my best friend.

Sunday, 5th

Today has been a very strange day and I feel that it is not over—not even remotely. It is only eight-forty-five in the evening and my body is in a state of agitation, enough so that Denver mentioned it when we went out to dinner. Young Caden was there. He looks healthy. Maybe we will finally have an athlete in this family. His head is square and his shoulders are broad. I asked what Denver's husband does, and she said something in agriculture.

It's nice to know that if I ever need to be put in a home, someone in this family will have enough money to do it.

Going back to Quang tomorrow for a follow-up, and then to get a referral to another office so I can start on Zyprexa. According to the Internet, Seroquel is not a good fit for me, anyway.

Wednesday, 8th

I'm not feeling the best anymore. My body has too many things in it right now. My blood did not even clear the first drug, now I have two in my system. My limbs are rigid. I called Bobby to help me grocery shop.

We talked about his mother, not Carol. Well, for a little while we did actually talk about Carol. She is not doing well financially. I can't help. Maybe the agricultural husband can.

Saturday, 11th

After four sleepless nights, I've decided to flush my medicine. There is something about watching a hundred, colorful little pills swirling down the drain that will give you a new lease on life. Whether this lease is healthy or toxic, we will see. If anything… I miss Tawny.

Wednesday, (scribble)

As if by the grace of the Lord himself, I've found myself encumbered with another visitor! Poor Rhea, with her curls and whatnot! She looks just as good as her mother. Just as healthy. She looks alive

(scribble)

Farron - enamel pins, Husqvarna, $400

Bobby - TV, Fitbit, paintings, $400

Denver - house

Caden - $250 (SAVINGS)

Sarah - China, T's jewelry, $500

Terry - watches, T's clothes, $600

I, Caden Leahy, an adult residing (pen runs out of ink)

Francine & Corey : *Part One*

A white SUV titters away from the exterior of a

three-story building constructed of reflective glass and steel.

Francine musters a weak wave to her driver, a young man

contracted by a rideshare application. During the twenty-minute

ride, he spoke to her about his inability to complete any

assignment given to him by his professors. She could not

empathize but reassured him in a gentle voice that everything

will fall in place. Almost twenty years ago, the woman did

rather well in college even if she had started later than she

would have liked.

With a crutch under each arm, she hobbles to the front

door where she is required to press a button to send an inaudible

alert to someone at the front desk. A petite girl in a yellow cardigan smiles and unlatches the door with a simple response of a switch.

Clumsy movements caused by a pair of over-cushioned huaraches makes her look foolish and incapable when it takes her double the time as a normal client. When she passes the front desk, the assistant's mouth falls into a loose V-shape. The girl's words break through her lips like the last few drops of a leaky showerhead. "Good morning, Mrs. Adams. I've already let Dr. Greene know that you're here."

"Mm-kay," Francine says, pairing the response with a sweet but fake laugh. She is not interested in speaking to some prissy, judgmental woman whose education was probably bankrolled by her father. A black BMW idled in a reserved parking spot and can be seen just by looking out of the window. There is no reason why a twenty-two year old needs a vehicle like that. "Thank you."

The woman decides to stand instead of wasting her time by lowering herself into a chair that could barely fit her own buttocks. For the last two months, this has become a common practice.

Priya, the straight-haired assistant with the posture of an android, does not invite the sour woman to sit. She just hopes that Dr. Greene will show up and his cinnamon-inspired cologne will wash the room from the scent of Francine's sinister ointment, or, perhaps, diaper rash cream judging by her bloomed panty lines. Priya never knew the details and she is fine never knowing for sure.

A flatscreen television plays a commercial for a new children's show. Sentient plants speaking to each other and having adventures, dragging themselves by their leaves. One clip shows a plant who is yellowing and ill. The upcoming episode is a clever guise for promoting proper hydration.

Dr. Greene's voice calls for the woman. His rich baritone fills the room like water flooding the hull of a sinking ship. Francine exerts a sigh and paddles her way past the man and down the hallway where his office sits at the end. Priya shoots a look to the doctor: temporarily widened eyes, a double-chin present. He returns a glare that is both admonishing and affirming before slipping behind the wall and out of sight.

-

Refusing his help, Francine lowers herself onto a wide and stiff futon. She rests her crutches against the cushion next to her. They slide to the floor with a muffled clatter and she waves it off. "I'll get 'em later."

"If you're certain," Dr. Greene says. He settles into his chair and pulls up a fold-out table to store his papers. "Give me one… Moment."

Francine nods once with small, residual bounces of her head until he initiates the session by asking how she has been. "Nothing's really happened, Doc Greene. Two weeks? Not a whole lot can happen."

"I see. Have you kept up with your journal?"

"Yeah," she clears her throat with a stuttering ticker. "I have."

"Is there anything in there that would indicate otherwise? Maybe something *did* happen and you've forgotten." His tone is gentle, like a brother coaxing his little sister. Their rapport has always felt that way to her. She sought him out due to the fact that they are neighbors and have been aware of each other for over a decade—before, during, and after the infection. "Would you like me to take a look, or should we just leave it alone for now?"

She cracks a smile. Her teeth are stripped of plaque and semi-translucent. One of her great and terrible habits is to brush her teeth out of boredom or when the feeling of losing control of her autonomy occurs. Within the depths of a beige bag nestled between her thighs is an unopened toothbrush and a cheap, half-empty tube of toothpaste. Dr. Greene is yet to be aware of this habit. In her mind, she is but a shining example of cleanliness.

"Y'all can leave it alone. Soon, though. Maybe." Francine pauses. "I'm not done with it."

He nods in an apparent understanding. "When will you be done?"

"When every page is filled up, otherwise it won't make sense. Y'all can read the first page, second page, whatever, but it won't be a good story."

"You're writing a story in your journal?"

The woman straightens her posture and raises her chin. "You told me to use it when I want to lay out my feelings all neat and tidy. Best way to do that is through a story, tellin'

people my story."

Dr. Greene leans back in his chair and crosses his hands

over one another. "I agree with that with all of my heart,

Francine. When you believe your story is ready, I would love to

read it."

"Don't you have a book?"

"I do." He can feel the presence of his first copy

radiating behind him. It is tucked on a shelf that hangs above his

closed laptop betwixt a collection of older leather-bound books.

Hegel, *Greene*, Fuller.

She does not expound beyond this observation. Her

fingers drum along her bag. It is frayed along the bottom and

she has taken it upon herself to peel the top layer of material

away from the faux-leather. Every session, the bag arrives in a

furthered state of disarray.

He points this out with a perfectly shaped cuticle. "Has your anxiety lessened at all since starting the journal?" Francine shakes her head. The expression on her face might as well say *duh*. "It'll take some time. Maybe you should have another journal just for triggers and emotional shifts."

The woman shrugs with a click of the tongue before diving into her bag to fish out a college-ruled notebook. It is flimsy and more worn than he had expected. Either Francine has owned that particular copy for a while or she has been using it more than he expected.

Francine holds up the book and wags it. "Started using it for triggers and what-not, then got carried away. The whole back"—she flips through each page and Dr. Greene attempts to identify any words or symbols drawn—"is my story. The whole timeline. One day, it's gonna be my book."

"It looks like you have a lot done! But, you know something, Francine?" His tone causes her to retreat the journal.

"You should start by sharing your story with me. We've talked about your anxiety, your sister and niece, but not your experience with the infection. You can get a fresh take on your writing and maybe I can give you a few pointers while we're at it."

With a starved breath, her eyes shut like a feather cast from the sky. "Uh-huh." The volume of her voice is low. "I know, I know."

"It's the reason why you're here. The reason for most of your newly manifested distortions. I'm sure you realize that. We outlined it in the packet during our first session."

"Yeah, I do."

"Okay, then. If it's easier, you can open up your journal and read from it."

Dr. Corey Greene had expected to come into this session and tackle the relationship between Francine and her sister. His notes were lined with questions and talking points. There was a system to untangle the mess inside of her head and he had thus far been delicate. However, her gumption invited him to navigate his methods at a different velocity.

It looks as if she took to it.

Francine drops her bag to the floor and squeezes it between her heels. The notebook opens up without a crack, the spine well-worn.

Her armpits were drenched from stale heat and a lack of formidable AC in her LLV—a blocky mail truck with hard seats, a wonky brake, and a creaking metal fan. The blades rattled with each rotation and if they weren't contained by a cage, Francine Adams would have been in fear of her life.

The heat penetrated the hull of her vehicle and exacerbated the scent of cardboard and ink within the sweltering chamber. Her cell phone played a live-feed from a local radio station, the audio fed into a Bluetooth speaker tucked into one ear. "We just gotta make it through the week, folks. The wave will dissipate by Saturday when northern winds…"

Her vehicle swooped into its next destination, a tight-knit apartment complex with three buildings and three subsequent drop-offs. Two shirtless men leaned over the railing of their second-floor home. They talk to each other with sweat pouring down their faces. Their glossy necks and shoulders garnered a blush from the sun that arched overhead and bombarded the Earth with its unrelenting assault.

One of the men lifted his hand to wave to her. She did not notice it as her job took priority with the news a close second. He waved once more, this time with an empathetic shout, and Francine looked up with pressed lips. The man asked with a raised voice, "You got AC in there?"

She cackled and completed her first drop-off. When the woman walked away and traversed between the two buildings that led into a courtyard, the men could see how drenched her back was. The light-blue clothing indicative of the USPS was stained a rich, navy blue. New, uninvited spots formed throughout the rest of her shift.

-

"I remember that June," Dr. Greene places his pen on the table and stretches his dominant hand. "They kept saying 'It'll get better, it's gonna get better'."

"Uh-huh. Same month everything went to shit." Francine sniffs and idly flips through the pages. "You know what, let me skip ahead a li'l bit."

"Well, what happened? Did those guys do anything to you?"

Her eyebrows curl like two surprised caterpillars. "Why would they?" She catches herself about to spoil a key moment in her potential book. "Spoilers—one of 'em comes back later, but, nah. Neither of 'em did anything but ask if I had any air conditioning in my truck."

Dr. Greene expresses his understanding with a non-verbal smack of the lips. He wants to make sure that every detail given is relevant in some way. If she is going to publish a book based on her story, he might as well give practical writing advice.

She looks up from her notebook. "Yeah, I'm—I'm gonna skip ahead just a bit. You okay with that?"

"I don't have a preference either way, Francine. It's your story, so tell it how you wish."

It is as if all of the gravity ever known to exist rested on top of her head. This decision to rearrange her words, the timeline, threw her into a moment of heavy unease. After a series of deep breaths to clear her mind, she recites from the mess of scribbles that are marked in her journal.

"'It was then that I received a phone call from my best friend and fellow *United States Postal Service* employee Tricia.'" Francine looks up from the page for approval. Without receiving any form of a reaction, she remembers that there is no need to depend on someone else to affirm her experience and continues with an air-bubble in her heart.

"Girl," an excited voice said through Francine's earpiece. "I saw him again, lookin' out the window with that big ol' coffee cup of his. Peekin' through the blinds, I saw him just—he was taking a big sip and starin' at me right in the eyes. I know he saw me lookin' at his dick. Franny, you can't miss that shit."

While climbing out of her vehicle, Francine snorted and shook her head. She made her way to the back while listening to her friend describe the event while lingering on as many details as possible. They spoke every day as long as they worked the same shifts. If one had the day off, they'd respect the other's privacy and catch them up the day after.

"Nothing like that ever happens to me," Francine sucked on her lips and threw the back door open. The middle of her shift always brought with it the most intense heat of the day. Stagnant air unleashed itself and swallowed her. "Damn. This *heat*, girl. I'm gonna drive off a cliff."

"Ain't no cliffs here."

"Oh, I'll find one. I-10 is just as good." She dragged a container filled with Priorities to her chest. The woman was able to sort through the lot with laser-focus. One envelope developed a dark spot in its left-hand corner. Francine brought it to her nostrils. "I think someone put a mouse in a two-day."

Tricia took a moment to respond. "Wait, what?"

"Smells like death. Oh, what the hell?" She checked the address and knew it was residential. Her current location was an industrial yard where shipping containers and loading docks made her feel like she was in the middle of a horror movie. Without any shade, unfettered heat swarmed the woman.

"Toss that shit," her friend suggested. The tone in her voice shifted to preoccupation. A wet chime sounded from her electronic signature device, though it sounded rather distant and hollow through the speaker. "Last name?" The question was not for her.

Francine set off to finish her deliveries. One building required a doorbell to be rung and it took a stocky, manic gentleman a full minute to say good-bye to whomever it was he spoke to over a corded telephone and answer her hail.

He opened the door for her and smiled. A shine licked his forehead, though the building had proper air conditioning.

While waiting for his shaky signature to be completed, she figured that she would rather feel hot than to stay in a frigid office all day.

She kept her eyes on the man. A thick ring of hair orbited his head with unkempt eyebrows and nose hair to match. Dark brown, almost black, eyes. When the stylus was returned, he wiped his drenched hands on his slacks and wished her a pleasant day.

If Francine didn't know better, she would guess that there was someone with a gun under the table. As much as she wanted to ask if he was okay, the woman figured that whatever he had going on was in no way her business. She moved to a dock next door and stopped an employee in the warehouse who, too, was covered in sweat. No strange business with him.

The call between her and Tricia had dropped at some point as it often did when they were caught up in their jobs. She called her friend back. "People are crazy." No response—again, not unusual. Francine headed back to her vehicle when a blip of her friend's voice squeezed through the speaker. "What's up, Trish?"

"Girl," she started in a whisper. "No shit people are crazy. This girl straight up looked like she was finna keel over and die just now." Francine recalled the balding man and reiterated her experience. "Kind of, but like, her eyes—oh, and her *breath*, Franny."

"Don't think anything was wrong with my guy's breath but, yeah, actually, his eyes did look creepy as all hell. Empty. But," the woman heaved a shrug. "That's what happens when you don't drink water durin' a heatwave." She started the engine and pulled out of the complex with one swift motion.

A group of homes were on the opposite side of a fence that divided the perimeter. Francine turned into the right-hand lane and took a moment to look back at the industrial yard.

The feeling of working in an environment like that had always terrified her. Something about the emptiness between buildings, that hot asphalt, and the claustrophobic feeling of spending most of her day behind the walls of an under-decorated cubicle gave her goosebumps. Her father, a man who had earned her respect as both a provider and an author of poetry, began his career as a copywriter whose office sat just outside of a similar complex.

When Francine crossed into the neighborhood, she was relieved to see the standard fare of children playing outside while the smell of barbecued meats wafted between each house. A thin plume of smoke dissipated into the endless sky from behind a quaint one-story home with an attempt of a succulent garden outside of its living room window.

She slowed her vehicle once she spotted a small dog off of its leash—a particular but warranted pet peeve as her older sister's dog was run over just a year after Francine was born.

Its wiry tail hung low and its nose traveled along the air to pick up a scent. With a smirk, she figured it wanted whatever was being grilled. A low rumble in her gut suggested the same for herself.

"Someone's cookin' some good ass food right now," Francine took in a breath of air that was stained with the odor of charred meat. Her senses were tricked into believing that she could pick up the taste. "Might just pop out for a sec and try to find Master Chef."

"Remember when I lived in Belmont?" She did not. "I don't even know if I told you about that time in my life. Oh, girl, you would have hated me. You could find me hittin' every bar from Gretna to New Orleans say, what, three years ago?"

Francine stopped at an intersection. "Before Josh," she said with a definitive tone. Her friend affirmed this with a pleasant hum. "Yes, ma'am. Luck hits you left and right."

"Oh, please."

"You start your day off with Mr. Bulge! Mr. Sexy-Big-Dick-Coffee-Cup. I had two gay Cubans dripping sweat on me from their patio." She parked next to a cluster of mailboxes and rolled out of her vehicle with a grunt. "I want a Mr. Bulge in my life. Shit, I'd even take a *Josh*."

Tricia hissed but did not gather a response. Francine figured that she had come on a bit too strong and allowed her friend a few moments to decompress. After some point, she broke the silence. "You good? Didn't mean to call you out."

"Actually," she made a pensive clicking sound with her tongue. "I'm watchin' some shit go down right now. I think I gotta—yup, okay. Hold up." The call disconnected and Francine pouted.

This is not the first time that either of them witnessed a display of domestic abuse while on the job. If this was not the case, then whatever stole her friend's attention would be explained at some point. Every detail, too, whether she liked it or not.

After delivering the few parcels meant for this block, worry began to creep up on her—the sound of dry paws against hot concrete was an audible example. She turned to spot the same dog following its curious route. It was panting to stay cool as its paws raised higher with every additional step.

Francine tried to get a look at the underside of the creature's pads. She hypothesized that they had blistered from the concrete. How the poor dog kept its head low with its staggered pace whelmed her with empathy. Snatching up the animal and keeping it safe in her un-air conditioned vehicle made just as much sense as leaving it alone.

The woman slipped the phone from one of her deep pockets and hovered over the browser icon. She backed out and instead chose to navigate her recent contacts.

The tip of a fine-point pen rests on Dr. Greene's lower lip. "You called Tricia instead of animal control?" Francine slumps in her seat and exhales a quiet, remorseful sigh. In so little words, she explains how she cracks under the pressure of morality. "And you think Tricia would have the answer for you?"

"My guiding light, my ride-or-d—"

"You should say it." He offers this suggestion with a casual smile. Dr. Greene senses her hesitance and relaxes his shoulders. Both hands sit on his lap to show his patience. "Francine, I think you would feel a lot better if you said it."

She shakes her head, not in dismissal of his request but in disbelief towards his attitude. "Nothing fazes you. You sit there all day listening to people's shit and you don't even bat an eye."

"Yes, well," he raises his eyebrows and breathes out a shallow laugh. "You can thank my therapist for providing me with an arsenal of healthy coping mechanisms."

The concept of a therapist receiving therapy had never occurred to Francine. She stares ahead like a deer caught in headlights. The longer she sits with it, the less unusual it becomes. "Do you talk to him about what we say?"

"No. I don't breach our trust." Or the law, he mentally adds. "I speak with her about my childhood and the stress I had in school. More recently, we talk about the infection."

"You suffered, too." Her tone is flat while sorrow wraps around the latter half of her sentence with a vice grip. Dr. Greene shows his perfect smile, his raised cheeks wrinkling the corner of his thoughtful eyes.

He does not say anything else and instead motions for her to continue reading from her journal. When Francine looks down at the pages and finds where she had left off, the desire to read his collection of thoughts, his story settles in her throat.

The words can not be spoken into creation. Even if they could,

she knows the therapist would never take a chance to damage

their relationship by making him appear human.

Francine & Corey : Part Two

Even as he prepares to speak, his face seems wooden.

"I don't know a single soul who hasn't suffered in one way or another, Francine," Dr. Greene says. "And many go through multiple trials throughout their lives. Some never suffer until something like this happens." His eyes fall to the sheets in front of him.

Several pages dictate a timeline in which to help his client heal. She watches him with swollen eyes and hunched shoulders. "It all comes tumbling down." The therapist cocks his browline up in agreement. "Okay. I'm ready if you are."

He did not have a choice. "Thank you."

~*~

Tricia answered with breathless haste. "What the fuck?"

"Uh," Francine stammered. The dog became wise and tapered off into the grass where it was marginally cooler. She felt less of a concern for the creature and more for her friend. "You good?"

"What the fuck is going on, Franny?"

The woman's voice popped in and out of the tinny speaker with every step of her long stride. She muttered to herself but the enunciation was lost due to the headset's poor quality. A cheap piece of plastic that did not contour to the inside of her ear. Francine pressed it deeper into the canal as if this would help renew clarity.

Two bumps, then the clanking of metal. Tricia said, "Where are you right now?"

"Not far from the Pig. Like, ten minutes." Francine fought with her roles as both a postal service employee and a devoted friend. She could not partition any attention to the buckets of envelopes and packages that still remained in her truck. The woman had never heard Tricia's tone of voice falter from being anything other than carefree. "Girl, what the hell is wrong with you?"

The friend, hidden inside of a cheap Bluetooth headset, calmed herself down with loud and quivering breaths. "I—hold up, sis. I got to *breathe*." A few moments passed and Francine found herself returning to autonomy. The back of her vehicle was stale, and with the addition of adrenaline flooding through her system, the smell that she carried with her even on her days off hit her as hard as an atomic bomb.

Tricia groaned, then squeezed out a pained squelch. "Okay. Franny, I just saw a man eat another man's face."

"Bath salts." Francine shook her head in slow berths. Her friend interjected just as she was going to continue speaking.

"No! Hell no! I know that shit—you *know* I know that shit. I have never seen anything like this before in my life. It was like a horror movie. Damn near crapped my shorts, girl!"

She closed the sliding door and hung onto the handle for a moment. "Did you call the cops?"

"I'm not callin' any cops. You know I handle justice by my lonesome." Her voice had returned to a level of stability that helped ease Francine back into reality. "But, you know I ain't touchin' this, which means I'm gettin' the hell out of here."

Francine started the vehicle back up and drove a short distance down the street and to the right. Along the route, she searched for the injured dog. A child was in an inflatable pool unsupervised. Tricia's voice dialed back in with: "You there? Did a man eat your face, too?"

Somehow, this was not funny. "No. I'm, uh, looking for a li'l puppy."

"Oh, I'm sorry. You sound distracted. Does my near-death experience *bore* you? I said I'm leavin', Franny. Takin' this bitch back to base and tellin' them I'm usin' a sick day."

"Nah, don't do that. You'll get your ass fired faster than Vernon."

"Don't curse me like that." Tricia clicked her tongue. "Are you seriously lookin' for a dog right now? We can go to Furever Home if you're so desperate for attention. Hell, I gotta get a few drinks in me after seeing that shit…"

Francine shook her head and exhaled a deep sigh gestated from irritability. Her right hand reached towards the earpiece and ripped it away. She could still hear her friend's voice from the other end. One light toss later and it rested in a compartment behind a pair of broken sunglasses.

The tight space only enhanced the sound that came from the small speaker. She tuned out Tricia like a mild case of tinnitus, her eyes kept to each yard they passed.

Adorable homes with wide porches, rocking or fold out chairs, hanging wind chimes with rods that tickle each other from the imperceptible breeze.

The dog had vanished.

When she parked and exited the vehicle, the smell of charred meat had mutated into burned flesh. The plume of smoke filtering upwards was darker on her second look.

Her appetite left her. The atmosphere of the neighborhood had never felt this way in the past. People should be relaxing on their patios, smoking cigarillos and drinking Arnold Palmers.

An old man whose wife had recently departed spent most of his day under the shade of his porch. Francine hoped that when she dropped a package off to his neighbor, he would

be waiting there to greet her with a cordial tip of his
Korea-Vietnam Veteran hat.

She almost spoke to reply to her friend's voice that no
longer resided in her ear and stopped herself with a huff.
Instead, the woman muttered something under her breath and
picked up her pace. After the next hasty drop-off, she reached
for the earpiece and tucked it back into place. "Trish?"

No response—the call was dropped yet again. Seconds
later, her cell phone rang. "Trish, you good?"

"You gotta meet me at the Pig. Okay? Fran—"

"Yeah, yeah. I got you. You safe?" That word fell from
her mouth like an anvil onto her foot. *Safe.*

Tricia paused, then said, "I will be. I'm fifteen minutes
away, comin' the opposite way. You good to meet me?"
Francine's tone shifted to panic.

"Yes, girl. I'm already on my way."

Nothing was ostensibly wrong. There had been no events on her end to convince her to abandon her post, but her friend's story of a man eating another man's face had not left her. It is as if a switch lying deep within her DNA was flicked on after a lifetime of being dormant. Even if she were to spend some time alone, Francine does not think she could come up with a reason as to why running just felt right.

"Stay with me 'til we meet up." Tricia squeezed this request out of her closed throat. "I feel like my heart is, like—*pat-tat-tat-tat-tat.*"

"Okay," Francine started, her brain searching for any words that made sense. "Just—tell me what happened."

"I was by the park, the one with the crazy long trail. I'm at the gazebos, right, and there's some birthday party thing goin' on for kids, and… Oh, Jesus." Her story became cold and a heavy sigh followed. "Cops are up here."

Francine could hear the sirens whip by her friend's vehicle. The sound came so quick and so loud that she felt the compulsion to throw the earpiece out of the window. After what seemed like forever, the strident sounds subsided. "Think my ear's bleeding. Christ."

"That was, like, ten cop cars. Holy shit. Oh, I feel like my gut is gonna burst. I have the nervous poops."

She laughed despite Tricia's sincerity. "You gotta calm down. I'm here with you." A moment of silence while both of them relax into their immediate reality. The road ahead of her rolled under the vehicle. Each light still worked as it should, though there was a significant increase in traffic as she closed towards the market district.

-

"Did you feel—how should I say this? I suppose, did you feel guilty for abandoning your post, so to speak?"

Francine contorts her lips. "Well, yeah. You know, I like to work hard. I like to give my job the respect it gives me."

"Were you confronted by any of your managers?" Dr. Greene is curious as to how his client handled such extreme stress.

When the news of the infection became public knowledge, his experience with the trauma surrounding it had already been solidified. He missed a day of work without giving any form of advanced notice. The guilt he once sat with still irritates him in waves.

She chortles and shifts in her seat. The strap of Francine's bag is caught under her cast, but it does not bother

her. "Shit hit the fan a day later, Doc. You were there, I'm sure. You know how it went down."

Dr. Greene feels a vibration in his right pocket. An alarm he had set for an hour blared in secret. He nods. "Yeah, I do know. Francine, our time is up for today. I want to thank you so much for sharing your story with me."

"But, wait—I'm not even done yet." She scratches behind her ear. "Can I pay for another hour?"

"I mean, it's my lunch," he laughs through his discomfort. "I gotta eat. If you'd like, we could make our meetings weekly instead of bi-weekly?" Francine rolls her eyes. At the risk of offending her, he eases an idea to the woman with a kind tone. "As far as I know, your schedule is pretty open."

"Y'all can eat right now. I won't judge."

"I'm—I didn't bring any food, Francine. I'm actually going out to meet someone."

"Oh, yeah?" Her attitude shifts. She rotates her face so that one eye locks onto him. "A lady friend?"

Dr. Greene forces laughter. The two have not yet established a relationship in which they could parlay humor. Regardless, he appreciates the effort and decides to humor her. "Lady friend, yes. It's been a while since we've met up."

"You sound nervous."

"It's… You've got me. It's a possibility."

Francine waves her hand and leans back into the comfortable cushion. "Ah. You got this."

-

Ever since he spoke of the Day Zero heatwave with his client, Corey Greene has become hyper aware of the sun and its aggressive candor.

He stands outside of an underpopulated health-oriented cafe with a focus on ayurvedic teas. It has been almost a week since he has had his last kombucha. Knowing that he would meet his ex-partner at the same place they first met has spawned a healthy amount of anxiety that he attempted to twist into excitement.

After saving the date a week prior, he avoided this street entirely—even though the detour added another three-to-five minutes on to his drive.

Corey had ordered from Yantra only twice since meeting Monica: once over the phone and once, in person, with his sister. He had her try Yerba Mate, to which she gagged and spat out the mouthful onto her vegan panini.

"You really drink this sewer water?"

Every time he drinks Yerba Mate, his mind runs over the incident. At first, it was funny to look back at this moment. He would smile over his can or glass and look like a fool laughing by his lonesome. After two years, though, the man wished that the memory would leave him. "Sewer water," Betsie called it.

"At least I didn't have you try kombucha."

"Will it make me trip?" He laughed and explained the process and benefits of fermented tea. She liked it more than the other beverage.

Corey's eyes are dulled over as he leans against the brick wall to the right of the entrance. A few people have exited the building since his arrival. He smiles and nods to them, maybe even wishing them a good day. If Monica were to see this, their meeting could actually start off on the right foot.

He sees her car drive by in the opposite lane. Okay, he thinks. It looks like she's coming from downtown now. Maybe she moved, so we can talk about that. Same car—it was old even when we were together, now…

The man shakes his head. Corey had made a promise to himself that he would not approach this with any negativity. If she was still driving her car with the janky stick-shift and torn

seats, that was her choice.

With a deep breath and a dab of his forehead, he starts

off towards her direction. She was either heading to the parking

lot or was daring enough to parallel park in front of the

restaurant. In any case, he will be waiting for her.

-

Mid-week strolls upon Francine with a quick pace. A

few more days and she will be back in Dr. Greene's office. On

the night of their last session, she sent an email to confirm an

upgrade to meet on a weekly basis. He responded minutes later:

"Francine, that is great news. See you on Monday."

His signature was minimalistic but obnoxious. There was

an image file of wild loops and strokes. Francine traced her nail along the lines while sitting at her desktop. If she were a worse person, she could probably forge a prescription.

A notification pops onto the lower right-hand corner of her screen and the cursor whips to open the message:

Fran,

Just trying to see that if you are good to take care of Amanda tomorrow morning 830AM. Please dont cancel, I need to be in N.O. by 10. I will drop her off around 830. Please just email me back and say yes. You dont have to say a anything else.

Lupi x

Even though she was not encumbered with any plans other than binge-watching television, the idea saddles her with dread. Being the godmother, she loves Amanda out of both obligation and genuine entrenchment after having invested the first six years of the girl's life as a recurring guardian. What was once an occasional sit became a full-time nannying gig after she lost her job with USPS.

Francine lifts her keyboard and drags her worn notebook out from under it. A nearby pen attaches itself to her hand and she flips through to find an unused page. This is a difficult task, but after an eventual conclusion, she scribbles: *Mandy is a BRAT. Guadalupe lets her do whatever she wants, eats whatever she wants. Piglet thinks I got money to eat fast food every damn day.*

A cleansing breath. She places the pen back to her right and crosses either hand over the opened notebook. The blanching glow from her email inbox illuminates the gestures of the woman licking her teeth. Francine shakes her head and rips the page out with an eye roll; she is careful to avoid watching herself perform this act.

The page is a ball, matted by her sweaty palms and rests next to the pen, idle until the white that swarms her head falls away to reveal clarity once again. This could take hours or days.

-

Francine wakes up two hours before the alarm on her clock wills her to. There is a curious fear that sprints through her body like a jolt of electricity, that of anxiety that she had somehow overslept and the child was alone in her living room or, even worse, still outside. She rolls to her side and looks out of the window. The only light that breaks through belongs to the moon.

The twilight is no reason for her to stay in bed.

Led by the promise of a dim nightlight, she slogs to the bathroom attached to her room. The darkness acts as a wall between her and the mirror. Even in such low light, she can see smudges, fingerprints, and areas where the glass had lost its luster. She turns on the light and embraces the shock of seeing herself.

While being forced awake so early in the morning, Francine does not expect to witness the usual verdure that blushes her cheeks after her first cup of coffee or ceremonial shower to start the day. The bags under her eyes weigh fifty pounds. Crust litters her eyelashes like pollen on the hood of a car.

The digital clock on her stove claims it is five-thirty-eight, but it has always been six minutes fast. Her rice cooker is still warm from her dinner the previous night. Fried egg, rice—that's it. As long as she is fed, she wants for nothing.

Her patio becomes a place of respite until the first sign of traffic shows itself. Cool air transmutes into a lukewarm hug until the sun breaks over the horizon and begins to warm her enough to flee inside. Having left the sliding glass door open, the humidity follows her into the living room. Now that there is some semblance of illumination in her home, she can see the state in which she exists.

An uneven pile of magazines that grew with every other drop-off from her former USPS co-workers. Two empty cups that once contained water, a plate with crumbs. Blankets that were supposed to be decorative are pulled away from her closet and repurposed as a fort in which her comfort is in direct correspondence with how protected she feels. Used tissues caked with snot from a sickness that ailed her weeks ago are identical to the crumpled balls that were utilized for drying tears—indistinguishable from each other.

The next half-hour is spent cleaning up after her lag from the past month. This time period subjected her to lows she had never experienced before and thoughts that concerned her enough to seek therapy. Her television was her best friend, and since starting therapy, the remote collected more dust than usual.

A knock at the door. Francine closes her eyes, inhales through her nose, and exhales with a raspberry. When she answers, a smile showing all of her fragile teeth welcomes her niece.

-

When the temperature of the morning settles into an uncomfortable equilibrium during the afternoon, Mandy makes her first request. She was content to watch television for a few hours before restlessness set in. "Can we go to the park?"

"The park?" Francine is sitting next to her, scribbling into her journal with a dying pen. With a vigorous shake, she resolves to toss the useless instrument. "You wanna go out to the park, honey? It's so hot out."

"It's okay," the girl looks away from the screen that displayed the same animated series about plants as Francine caught a glimpse of just a few days before. "I don't mind."

The woman raises her browline. Her tone becomes stale. "Amanda, just because you don't mind don't mean I do." They stare at each other, her niece growing more irritable with every passing second. "I'm tired, baby. I didn't get any sleep last night."

Mandy turns back to the television. "Mama says that one too. No sleep, blah blah. Tired, too tired."

Francine blinks. "How often do you go out and do fun stuff with your mama?"

"Ne-ver!" The girl's nasal voice is muddled between tight lips. "All we do is watch TV and play fake bowling."

"You don't like video games?" Mandy pauses to think about this. She shrugs with a passive dismissal. "You wanna go to the park? Which one?" The girl's eyes light up and then harden within the span of a few seconds.

"We don't gotta go."

Francine does not respond. Her stare applies enough pressure that the girl feels obligated to explain. Mandy squeaks, "The one with the two lakes."

Francine nods, knowing the location well. "With that big wood jungle gym and the tire—"

"Tire swings! Yes!"

The girl launches herself onto the floor and squeezes her fists shut by her chest. Glee floods through her like a broken dam. Her interim guardian draws in a deep breath and wills herself up. "Well, it's gonna take a bit. I gotta get dressed and call a car."

She nods and offers a thumbs-up.

Without any hesitation, Mandy asks with a shimmering brightness: "It's okay, I can wait. Can we bring snacks?"

Francine had been waiting for the girl to mention food. "Yes, we can, but *I* get to choose which ones." This compromise is received well by the girl who was already making her way to the kitchen.

Her niece stops in her tracks and spins on her heels. Comfortable socks with grips on the bottom prevented the child from falling. "Okay, then. You choose. Can there be brownies?"

Francine watches the girl pace around the house while humming an unfamiliar tune in which lyrics occasionally break through. Piecing it together, she figures it is the theme song to the ridiculous plant cartoon she was subjugated to watch.

She lifts herself from the couch, mindful of her still-broken foot, and claws at her crutches that lay on the armrest next to her.

-

All of the swings are occupied by other children who believe they deserved it more. If it were up to Francine, she would instate a five-minute block of time for anyone using the limited equipment found at Mandy's favorite park. No one needs to be swinging for more than five minutes, she rolls her eyes.

"Can't you tell them to get off?" The girl hugs her chest tight. Her shoulders are hunched and stiff. "I need a turn."

Francine searches the other side of the playground. "Look there. Nobody's on that one slide. Go have fun over there for a bit. Mandy, don't give me a face. I'll call you when this swing is free."

"You promise?"

She closes her eyes and nods. A short sigh is exerted by the young girl who decides that the slide could potentially be as fun as swinging. Her steps are slow at first before breaking into a sprint with a giggle. Francine keeps her attention between the two attractions.

A pre-teen boy idles on a swing, his attention glued to his phone. She approaches him with a limp that suffers worse with uneven terrain under her, careful to stay behind him and not in the trajectory of the other two children that act as pendulums. "Sir?" No response—earbuds are now visible under his mop of hair. With a grunt, she lifts a crutch and taps his shoulder. He jumps and frees his right ear.

"What the heck?"

"Do you mind if I take that swing for my niece?" Her eyes cast to the slide. For a moment, Francine can not find the girl. A gleeful shout reverberates through the plastic tube that births the child onto shredded tires.

"Um," the boy ruffles his own hair. It falls over his sleepy, blue eyes. "It looks like she's having fun over there, so…"

Francine grits her teeth. "Yes," she starts. "I understand how it could look that way, but there is something you have to understand. She's dying." He frowns and reassesses Mandy. From a distance, she looks to be in perfect health—if not just a little above the weight her pediatrician would like to see her at.

He blinks. "*Really?*"

"Yes. What's your name?"

His voice is like mud. "Tyler."

"Of course it is. Tyler, honey, do me a favor and go someplace else. She don't got much longer on this earth and every second we're talking is another second she's wasting."

How a woman with a broken foot, two crutches, and a decaying leather bag could look so intimidating was beyond him.

The pre-teen chews his upper lip and cocks his left shoulder. His phone feels heavy in his hand. With a tight nod, he lifts himself away from the swing and avoids being hit by a young boy on his descent.

She waits for him to be a fair enough distance away to call for her niece.

\-

Even in the sleepiest quadrant of New Orleans, the air was heavy with electricity and scents that woke the senses. Flavors that coat the air were chewed on between every word spoken between the patrons of a bar independent from the chaos just five minutes away. Stools squeak with every movement.

They do not turn as well as they first had decades ago, and the material is lifted and torn under them.

Corey examines his lowball glass and the inch of liquid that remains. The flat of Monica's palm rests on the space between his shoulder blades. She leans in and whispers something before laughing in the delicate way he nearly worshipped. His brow drops but a suspicious smile grows on his face as he tries to twist his seat to look at a couple behind him.

The sound of rusted metal scraping against each other alerts everyone sitting at the bar and the two men behind him. They catch Corey catching a peak and roll their eyes. He can not help but laugh. The man holds up his hand and mouths an apology while one-half of the couple giggle while calming his partner down.

A gentle push from Monica. "You botched it!"

"What was I supposed to be seeing?"

"The way they danced on each other. Those outfits!"

With another glance, Corey appraises the two. "They look damn good. What? I'm not trying to lie!"

"They do, they do." Monica settles in her seat. She reaches for his glass and finishes the last swig. Her tongue sticks out of her mouth and closes one eye in a reflexive gag. If she were not drinking, she would be more mindful to compose herself. "Jesus."

His smile is wide while his caramel eyes catch the light from surrounding neon signs. "Yeah, I didn't offer for a reason." After a short bout of coughing, she sniffs and reaches for the appetizer menu. Monica raises her thin, shaped eyebrows to invite him closer. "I could eat."

Their faces are close to each other, but she finds herself leaning into him. After a moment, their cheeks become pressed against each other. She enjoys the warmth that exudes from him. Corey's scent was that signature cinnamon and clove she found herself catching in the wild at the worst of times.

When she speaks, he feels her cheeks flex. "Remember when we broke up?" He nods but keeps the same pressure on her face. The bartender pretends not to notice when she passes by. "Can we just forget about it?"

Their skin detaches. He clears his throat and pulls the menu away from her. Chicken wings sound good. "No," Corey responds before the inevitable moment where she shuts down. "I don't want to forget about it. I want to enjoy tonight, but I don't want to ignore reality."

"The reality is that I'm sorry." She pulls the menu back but he catches it with the tips of his fingers. Monica frowns. "We're both at fault, you know. We both acted like children."

"Yeah, but, I don't want you to take all the blame."

"What do you want?"

His nostrils inflated. "You want to share some wings?"

The woman scratches her forehead and looks down at her outfit. Black, tight-fitting velvet. Sweat is trapped under her breasts, her crotch, and everywhere else. When she breathes, the smell of alcohol rises to her nostrils. Under her acrylics was a layer of concealer she peeled away. Monica uses the back of her hand to blend her damaged brow and says, "Might as well."

-

The back seat of an older Toyota Corolla has seen better days. Stains are hidden by loose-fitting seat covers that bunch under Francine and give her the feeling of a persistent wedgie. A growing agitation rises in her body like steam from a painful shower.

Just as she opens her mouth to speak, her driver catches her in the rearview mirror. His voice is nervous. "I do not really go to this part of town," Tayeb claims. She considers this obvious as he has missed two turns even when referring to his GPS every few seconds. "Many people have cars."

She pauses to assess him from the back seat. Hunched shoulders and white-knuckling the steering wheel. "How long've you been driving?"

"For the app?" Tayeb smiles, but she can not see it. "You're my fifth ride ever." For some reason, this made the woman nervous. She shifts in her seat and feigns enthusiasm through some automatic response that eludes her consciousness mere seconds after jettisoning from her mouth.

Francine peeks at her phone. Nine more minutes until she reaches the office.

The woman had been obsessing over her story since receiving an affirmation that the method is indeed a healthy way to process her trauma. Dr. Greene seemed especially enthused and had even offered to give her some writing and publishing tips. An idea drifts into her skull.

"Tayeb," she mispronounces his name yet he still responds. "I don't want to seem rude or anything"—he prepares himself for whatever bigoted nonsense is about to ensue—"but, how long have you been in the country?"

He nods to himself. A second-long pause to gather his bearings. "Twelve years."

"Oh, shit." The volume of Francine's voice drops. "That's—so, you've been around long enough for the whole Cat Scratch thing." She states this with an almost bitter but definite sense of morosity coating the back of her tongue.

The driver is taken aback by her question. His answer comes out slow. "Yes, ma'am."

"And you lost people?

"Yes, ma'am." The tension in his arms lessens. Tayeb flicks a turn signal and rubs his eye with the same hand before it finds its position back on the steering wheel. An additional reply is loaded into his mouth like a shell in a cannon. "You want to know the funny thing is? I still have cats. Two!"

Francine pulls the bag on her lap closer to her chest. "You have cats?"

"Two!" He shakes his head. A weak scoff exfoliates his throat. "Knock everything over. Chasing each other all the time, but very cute. Get in the way of prayer, too, but sometimes they sit with me and I…"

She does not think she could ever understand how anyone could ever own a cat after losing loved ones to the plague that manifested from their blood and through their nails, their teeth. Tayeb continues his story, but Francine only tunes in for the last half. "And I could not blame them, the police. I understood. You know?

"As soon as it all, erm—as everything settled down, I went to the Furever Home and asked to adopt and they looked at me the same way you look at me now. Disgust."

Francine pouts and fights with her lower lip to return back to its normal position. Her teeth grind against each other as she waits for him to continue. Two minutes left until she reaches

Dr. Greene's office. It becomes evident that Tayeb has no reason

to.

\-

Corey is nursing alkaline water from a matte white water

bottle when he is alerted about Francine's arrival. His brow

collapses downward until his eyes disappear under the strain of

his migraine.

~*~

In the middle of an overcrowded parking lot, two USPS

vehicles idled next to each other and took up multiple spots in

the far right corner. Sitting in the back of Francine's mostly

empty cargo hold, Trisha completed her detail-by-detail retelling of the assault. "He had no nose, girl. Chewed it like a piece of bubble gum."

"Jesus Christ." Francine exhaled. Sweat stuck to every inch of her body, and, yet, it did not concern her as much as it had an hour before. "I just gotta say, I don't feel right about that."

Trisha's head bobbed as she scanned her friend's face. "Can I tell you somethin'?" A slow, tired blink from the woman opposite her. "I know what this is. I know what it's gonna be."

"Okay."

She licked her lips and crooked her neck around the wall of the vehicle to see if anyone was near enough to eavesdrop. The woman threw a heavy exhale into the open air. "This is us gettin' murdered, Franny. Us. You know—*us*." Trisha gestured to her arms, her neck, her face.

"I don't—what are you saying?"

"The government hates us, wants to divide us. Yeah?"

Francine nodded. It was the easiest conclusion all day. "They want to keep us suppressed, they want us starvin' and fightin' each other. You know, 'black-on-black violence'. Ha!"

Francine rubbed her eyes with either palm. Her hands were dirty. The filth of the day had not yet been washed off. "What does this have to do with people eating each other?"

"You'll see, baby."

"Just tell me. Trish. If you got some ideas I don't, you have to tell me. Something don't sit right in my gut about this and I don't know why. I mean, you and I are sitting in the middle of a parking lot instead of doing our jobs. People won't get mail today 'cause of us."

Trisha massaged her thighs while consuming herself in deep thought. "You know those zombie movies? No, I'm not sayin' that's what these are, but—listen, girl. Some virus hits the population and the world scrambles around tryna figure out how the hell they're supposed to survive."

"Yeah, I know. We used to watch those Romero movies, me and dad."

"I don't know if it's gonna be that bad," Trisha said, her head moving with every word. "But, we're at the Pig right now. We got two big ass trucks. You feel me?"

Francine combed over the plan in silence, her friend allowing her the courtesy to do so without interruption.

One isolated incident was not enough to divert the course of her entire life. A frigid wave of guilt rattled her and she seethed while shaking the feeling off. As she turned to her friend, she was met with the screen of a cell phone.

Trisha said, "You in?"

A headline had just been posted about the very same incident. Francine grabbed the phone with one hand and scrolled through the article with the fingers from her other. "Da-da-da, officers at the scene were forced to... Okay, so they got him. No, wait, it says the first guy was already…" She shook her head and let go of her friend's phone. "Said the first guy was already dead, and a woman was acting out when they got there."

"And they shot the woman." Trisha said this with such pristine confidence, Francine began to panic. "If they didn't shoot the woman, she'd go around and find someone else to bite. Maybe it is like them Romeros after all."

The two hang their feet over the edge of Francine's vehicle. The longer they sat, the more time it felt like they were wasting. Trisha asked, once again, if she is ready to head inside and stock up. "A butt-load of water, a lot of beans. I'm talkin' like, a scary amount of beans. Oh, and we should get to the vitamin section and get cold medicine and Irish sea moss."

"Moss?"

"Iodine, girl. Just in case they drop a nuclear bomb and we're the only ones left!"

Francine's tone switched as she asked, "Am I staying with you?" This sobered Trisha who pursed her lips and shook her head. "I ain't got a basement in my apartment and I'm, y'know, alone and shit."

"I… You know, I can talk to him. I can try to talk him into it. Don't worry about that right now, Franny. Base is gonna be blowin' up our shit soon trying to find out why we're at the Pig instead of our route."

She nodded and understood that it would have to be a conversation between Trisha and Josh. Whether he would be open to the idea of *zombies* or some infection targeted at black communities would be another conversation altogether.

-

"That's quite an interesting theory," Dr. Greene admits while wincing at every throb that punches at the inside of his temples. "And one I've heard before."

Francine's eyes light up. "Really?" She leans forward with such haste that the bag between her feet spills over. An old clear plastic bag contains her toothpaste and brush. Minty scum cakes the interior. "Do you think it's true?"

"Well," he gathers himself and rubs his chin. "I'd say that with the… With all of the different sources from all over the United States—you know, as it came to be once the dust settled and Internet access was restored, sure. Many low-income, dominantly black areas were actually the last to receive restoration of power."

She flares her nostrils and nods. "Mhm."

Dr. Greene clicks his tongue then shrugs. "So, sure. Yeah, I'd believe it. What happened after that? You stayed with Trisha, correct?" It takes a moment for the woman to bring her thoughts back into a linear time frame.

"Yeah. Yeah, she managed to talk to Josh and he let me move my shit in."

"Were you able to go back to your apartment once everything was over?"

Francine's voice cracks when she tries to speak. He gives her a moment to breathe, and in the meantime scratches a note detailing her reaction. "I had to go back. Josh—that boy. I can't blame him, 'cause he didn't know."

"You'll have to be more specific. What didn't he know?"

"That the—those damned cats brought the sickness and his white knight-self tried to bring in a stray." The therapist shakes his head and scratches his forehead. A lump is caught in his throat.

"You're serious? So, you're saying that he put you both in danger—"

"Well, he didn't know, Doc. We didn't even know."

Dr. Greene calms himself with a long, therapeutic breath. He apologizes and looks back to the sheet on the foldout table between them. "Is it correct to say you watched them both succumb to the illness?"

With a rolling shrug, she sighs and slumps into her seat. "This hurts."

"Yes, it does, but it is also necessary. Let me ask you another question, maybe rephrase it a little: do you feel guilty?"

"Guilty?" She frowns. "Why would I feel guilty?"

"You tend to feel a lot of remorse about plenty of events in your life. Right? That's fair to say? We've discussed living in the past and bringing yourself to the present, so, do you feel guilty in the way that you feel as if you could have saved either of them?"

Her tongue drags along the back of her uneven teeth. A wordless tilting of her shoulder is the only response she can muster. Dr. Greene continues with, "It would have happened whether they invited you or not. It is Josh who has a caring, philanthropic personality from what you've detailed. Trisha, it seems to me, did not want you with them."

"I've thought about that."

"He was the one who invited you in and tried to rescue the cat, maybe to save it from the infected outside. It's—Francine, it's really hard to know what anyone is thinking, but we know that he died trying to be the best person he could be." She looks past him and to the book with his name printed on the spine. "As far as Trisha, she helped you understand the severity of the situation and wanted to save you in her own way. Imagine if you two hadn't been friends, where you'd be or if you'd be here right now."

The whites of her eyes are now blemished pink. Her voice is so delicate that he can barely understand her. The smacking of her lips as she crafts her words come through louder than their full enunciation. "Mm. Thought about that one, too."

"But, you knew you had to leave. You saw what was happening and left. Correct?"

"Right."

"You saved yourself, and that's not a bad thing or anything to be ashamed of. That's self-preservation. Imagine if you were Trisha or Josh for a moment. The last thing you'd want is to know that you killed your friend."

Francine closes her eyes and puts herself into the shoes of Trisha, and then her partner. "They just ended up killing each other. Josh—oh, good Lord. I feel sick."

"Okay, okay," Dr. Greene says. He begins a specific breathing exercise and invites her to join him. After a messy union, they both harmonize and relax together. "You're doing great. I can see how much better you feel. We do need to process this memory at some point, but we can stop for now. Is there anything else you'd like to talk about?"

Her eyes open back up to the world. A small but comfortable office. A handsome man. The book with his name on it. Francine's lips twitch. "H-how was your date?"

The man's bottom lip fattens when the attention is brought onto him. His tongue sticks to the corner of his mouth as he reminisces over the night. He feels no need to share the more intimate details with his client, but, upon returning his attention to her, genuinely cackles at the goofy expression Francine holds.

Lorelei Coffin : *Part One*

The most prized possession in Lorelei's home is a
thirty-eight inch television. It is flat and with a fairly decent
picture despite the device nearing a decade-old birthday. Digital
cable had been recently installed with the help of an
intimidating, blinking device that emitted so much heat that she
could barely stand to be around it for longer than a few
moments. Thanks to the small box, however, the channels she
could access increased triple-fold.

Unfortunately, none of them were too interesting.

She received updates from the world via the glowing
screen. When she woke up in the morning, the television would
already be on. Muted through the night, its flickering projection

danced across the floor, squeezed tightly under the crack of her door, and created a silent show for her to fall asleep to.

Though Lorelei Coffin was surrounded by neighbors to every side of her, she was terrified of being alone. Heightened moments of domestic abuse from the neighbors on B-208 kept her ears pinned to the wall during the evenings. A microwave meal or leftover takeout would be eaten in silence as she listened in on the latest of happenings from the couple to the apartment across from her. Two notebooks were kept nearby, one filled but used for reference, and the other on its way.

During her evening stretches, the neighbors across the courtyard could always find an occasion to party. Dance-hall music and a foreign, Slavic language. Children would roam the parking lot with a soccer ball, though they almost never properly played with it. Just a prop, she wrote in the second, green-faced and flimsy journal.

The evening before, she mutes her television a few hours earlier than she normally would and opens her mouth to speak. There is nobody in the room with her and there hasn't been for years. "I—I..." Her voice cracks, her throat parched. The woman's thin lips curl in rubbery gymnastics. "I love you, Vicky-kitty."

A monsoon of pent-up depression escapes her, her face melting with hot tears that seemingly come from nowhere.

-

Is my head full of ocean water? She jotted this down while tucked in her bed. A small, ring-light lamp illuminates her side of the bed with a pure white cascade. Lorelei catches herself staring directly in its center. The old woman closes her eyes and breathes in the image that is burned behind her eyelids—that of an intense halo.

Pride slowly filled her lungs like drowning in a vat of warm olive oil. She should have made a note as to when the last time she spoke was. Must have been a week, a voice concurrent with her own insisted. You went to Foodsmart and grunted at an employee.

Feeling confident, she replied, "Well, he deserved it. I should've found a damn manager. Eyeliner on a *man*, all clumpy and uneven." Lorelei placed the notebook down in her lap and rolled the pen over the surface.

His eyeliner wasn't bothering anyone.

"I'm not bothered by it. I don't care if a guy wants to wear makeup. Just, someone else out there—someone… Another customer could come in and look at that and feel very *disturbed*." The woman shook her head before tossing the pen to the floor. It did not make a sound as the plush carpet caught its weight.

It doesn't matter if someone else feels disturbed. You are living your own life, in your own apartment—

"Don't have a cat anymore. Don't have anybody out there to give a crap about me." Lorelei stares at the pen. If she were younger and more limber, it would already be back in her hand. The two-foot drop appeared to be a chasm as she felt her age squeeze her joints.

The voice chose not to respond this time. A sad buzz skirted the inside of her skull like a toy top with a slowly dying spin. It is no secret to anyone who has ever encountered Lorelei that she tends to look towards the negative in life; deals at the supermarket are never the right ones, reruns on her television are always the worst episodes. Throughout the day, she cursed at her own body, her own reflection.

You are not a victim, the invisible entity spoke once again. She nods and felt her bottom lip roll inwards before reaching over the side of her full-sized bed. The woman verbally wills her fingers to grow an extra inch, once again feeling the burden of her genetics trumping a menial, otherwise achievable task. Straining to capture the pen results in the woman toppling over and bumping her head against the nightstand.

There is silence in her room and on the television. An image of a colorful commercial featuring a nuclear family jubilantly bonding over a twenty-piece fried chicken meal caught her attention. A dull throbbing entered the spot on her head that should have immediately felt pain.

Her face is pressed against the carpet. From this angle, she can see a forest of tiny trees made of fabric knots spreading as far as the kitchen wherein tile finally eats the texture away. She wants to move, to sit up, to crack her knuckles and climb back into bed but her body is mostly frozen. Lorelei is able to move her toes and her fingers, but a paralyzing shock is still running through her body like currents of electricity powering someone's home.

After a moment, she regains the ability to speak. There is very little power behind her voice—just wisps of air. Along with it, a creaking chair, a loose floorboard. Shaking elbows, a lack of confidence of her own strength. A moment of hope and one of subsequent defeat. Frustration paints her face and tears well in her eyes.

Lorelei decides to just rest and watch the silent television. A rerun of a late-night sitcom is on, one she has seen more times than she can count. The woman plays a game with herself: guess the dialogue. After succeeding only a handful of times, her internal voice uses this as a method to engage with her.

You could starve down there.

"I've been through it before."

It's not like before. You were younger back then. You had Vicky and she was so, so loud.

With irritation, "She was fat. Even if I died on the floor, she would be okay." She allowed herself a moment to recall a sweet memory with her cat. Waking up in the early morning and having the cat perched on the cloth tower, staring at the door to her bedroom and hopping down to greet her once as soon as she saw the woman in her flannel nightgown.

There is no pressure behind her eyes yet the tears come as easily as wind over a stagnant lake. She can feel the material under her flesh become damp. Before Lorelei is cognizant of her next action, her mouth is already open and a widening bellow fills her apartment. No longer is it weak, like a typical negligible sound from a nosy neighbor, but it is strained with intention. A plea of help.

Think of Vicky, the voice suggested. Not that she's dead, but how absolutely *loud* she was. The woman downstairs used to slam her fist against the wall and shout for her to shut up. Be as loud or louder than Vicky. Let the world know you're—

A rapid succession of knocks on her front door connected from the living room. Lorelei quiets herself and feels how raw her throat has become. If she didn't know any better, blood might as well be coating her tonsils. A man's voice speaks with urgency, but the words are lost due to the distance.

Lorelei takes in a searing breath and comes to terms that she must continue asking for help. The physical presence of another human so willing to come to her aid is surprising, and the idea of human contact is equally as intimidating. Despite the fear—and there is quite a lot of it—the elderly woman bellows out once more: "Please, help!"

There is no response on the other side of the door, but there is a curious series of *clicks*. Lorelei can see the front door to her apartment gently swing open. A tall man with a crooked posture and a loping gait spots the woman and rushes into her room. "You're alright, ma'am," he says with straight enunciation that falls away from uneven and gappy teeth. His smile is kind and genuine.

He asks for consent to help her to her feet. She states that she is relieved that he managed to find a way into her locked home. "Maybe that's a conversation to have with the front office. Up you go, right here." The man crouches by her side while she sits on the edge of her mattress. He lets her catch her breath before asking her name.

"Lorelei," she blinks once. "Miss Coffin. No, no. You can call me Lorelei."

"Peter. It's nice to finally meet you."

The woman scans his unfamiliar face. The timbre of his voice does not resonate with any memories of the apartment complex. "Are you new here?"

"Oh, kind of. Two years on May fifteenth." He lowers himself into a cross-legged position and looks up at Lorelei with gentle but consistently teary eyes.

She shakes her head, visibly uncomfortable. "You can stand up now. I'll be fine." After a brief moment to consider her request, Peter clears his throat.

"Alright," he rises to his feet with minor difficulty. A dry groan tapers into a sigh. "Did you want me to leave?"

"How come I've never seen you before? Or heard you?" Lorelei shifts in her seat. The longer the stretched-out man stays in her space, the more a looming sense of discomfort grows.

His outfit is simple: a salmon button-up shirt with a stiff collar, loose slacks with the contrasting color of royal blue. A black belt without as much as a stretch mark on it. White socks hidden under his pants that lead to brown loafers with a rounded toe. No scent on him as far as she could tell, not that her nose was considered keen anymore.

The internal voice insists that the mysterious stranger is an alien sent to abduct her. How else could he have opened the door?

Peter is waiting for Lorelei to respond to him. He cocks his head. "Are you okay? Did you hear me?"

"Oh. No. What did you say?"

He laughs. It is choppy and quiet. "I just said that I like to keep to myself. I have family in town so I've been spending most of my time with them. My little sister, mostly."

The old woman frowns. Wrinkles appear all over her face. "You said all of that?"

"Ha! Not really. I added the part about my family and my sister." He rests his hands on his hips and straightens his back. She can hear a loud pop and winces. "Sorry. That's a bad habit of mine."

Lorelei does not look offended at all. "What, you have scoliosis?" They both share in a knowing nod. "You want some cream? I have some hot-stuff I put on my knees. Made out of—oh, ah… Capsaicin."

"Whew," Peter seethes and crosses his arms. "That's too intense for me." He takes in his surroundings without being obvious. She notices this and chooses not to mention it. Of all the rooms in her apartment, her bedroom is kept up the most.

If he asks to use the bathroom, the voice begins. Say no.

No amount of dust is allowed to settle on her bookshelf, her bedframe, or her nightstand. A long, plastic device with a wispy end is tucked near the corner of her bed. With what little energy she had left, she was happy to expend it on keeping her sacred space up to snuff.

The woman rubs the back of her head and feels a tender lump. With pursed lips, the man asks if she is injured. "No. I just bumped my head on the—on the thing. I'm fine. Listen, Peter," she places both hands in her lap and straightens her curved spine as much as possible. "Thank you."

"You want me to leave?" His words came across as more of a statement than a question. She shrugs with both shoulders and winces when a sharp pain stabs her neck. "No, I—I can't in good conscience do that. Look, I'll make a deal with you." The man looks around the room and pulls up a heavy wicker chest to sit on. "I'll stay here for one hour."

Through a scowl, "What are you, a doctor?"

"I'm not a doctor, but I do have some medical background."

"Just don't call an ambulance."

The voice chimes in: they'll probably try to kill you on the way to the hospital. Might as well let them.

Lorelei squeezes her eyes shut and shakes her head once to rid herself of the thought. This is a habit that has become more prevalent within the past two years.

Picking this tic up, Peter offers a calm smile. "I know. It's expensive. A ride to the hospital costs so much money nowadays." She can see the appearance of a shadowy beard that struggles to break through his pale skin.

Dryly, sans humor, "You think I'm poor?"

He half-expected a response of this caliber. "Even the rich can hardly afford healthcare nowadays. If you feel *so* offended by my presence, I'll leave!" He says this coquettishly as he readies himself to stand up. "You'll never have to see me again!"

She pats her tight, snowy curls worn as a crown and considers his offer. "You seem nice enough. You were right, by the way, so don't get any ideas." The woman performs one sweeping gesture to Peter's confusion. "I *am* poor. You look like you have a good job."

"It's—it's a desk job. You know? I have a little office, a minion who runs and gets me my morning tea…"

Not impressed, she springs forth the question: "Well, what is it that you do?"

His posture collapses inwards as he responds. "Government."

"Oh-h-h! So I can blame *you* for my being poor!" Peter watches her face for his next cue. He does not know whether to laugh or dive into a genuine apology. She flares her nostrils and rolls her eyes. "I thought you had a sense of humor."

"I do, I just didn't know if you did."

"Being a teacher for thirty years, you have to find the funny where there is none." Lorelei looks away from the man as bait. She waits for him to ask more about her past. Her mind is already busy dredging up old stories, clarifying all of the little details—names, dates.

Peter adjusts his stiff collar with a crooked finger. "Do you have a cell phone?"

Sobered, she answers, "A what? Why?"

"You fell," he relaxes his shoulders and fixes his eyes to her shrunken form. "And, let's just say if I wasn't here, you could have been there for a while." Lorelei accepts this with a loose nod and a teary glaze over her eyes. "So, you should probably think about getting a phone."

She scoffs. "Nobody's gonna call me."

"It's for you to call other people," the man says with increasing desperation. The usual monotony of his voice raises into heightened inflection. "So you can be safe. You can call me. I'll give you my phone number and you can text or call if you ever need help with anything or—"

The old woman shifts in her seat and looks away. "What next? You going to marry me?" He pouts and feels his limbs become rigid. A silence shared between the two breaks when she clicks her tongue to release a half-realized apology. "You're kind and all, but, really—I'm fine. I've gone through it before."

His head bobs in an elastic nod for a moment. "Yeah? How long ago was that?"

Without any hesitation, "Seven years ago."

Peter's face returns to its previous, soft phase. His uneven lips curl into a stale, toothy smile. "That's around Cat Scratch, huh?" Lorelei does not respond verbally, yet her eyebrows cock higher on her forehead, eliminating the pale space between her permed, white hair and beetle-like eyes. "You were younger back then."

"Not much."

"Do you feel old, Miss Coffin?" He scratches the top of his head, apologizes, and corrects himself. She can see several errant flakes of dandruff escape the clutches of his dry scalp. She mentally prepares herself to drag out the vacuum in the morning.

"I *am* old."

"Do you have children?"

She straightens her spine once again. "I don't feel comfortable talking to you anymore." A tight grin appears on his face. Lorelei frowns and pushes the air between them. "You're looking at me like a psychopath!"

"Sorry," he says through a quiet sigh. "I get that I can come off a little strange. A little 'too much'. People tell me that all the time."

The woman crosses her arms and tucks them under her breasts. "Well, you do."

Exhaustion settles onto his face. A full shift of working in a drab office is enough to drain anyone. He expected to kick off his shoes and melt into the couch. The image of his apartment—perhaps just as dreary as his cubicle—fades into the forefront of his mind and a dull sense of longing trails behind it.

Peter scans the woman once last time. "Are you tired? Sorry. Just a few more questions. Are you tired?"

"I'm always tired."

"I get it. I'm just afraid that you may have a concussion, so I'm just trying to keep your mind occupied." The pale gentleman crosses his legs and straightens his spine to the best of his ability. His empty apartment will be fine without him. The leftover pasta in his refrigerator will still be edible. After another inaudible but held sigh, "So, if it's okay with you, I'm just going to stay here for a little while. I'm not going to call an ambulance unless I see you having any symptoms."

Lorelei rolls her eyes, still uncomfortable with maintaining eye-contact. "Not unless you want to pay for it."

His strange chuckle fills the room. It is always twice as loud as his speaking voice. "I don't. I really don't. So, Lorelei! No children?"

She weighs her responses with a coy smirk. "I've had hundreds."

"Your students?"

The woman glances at him with a proud gleam refracting the brilliance of her dark irises.

For a moment, she seemed young. The dim lighting of her bedroom erased a majority of the trenches on her face. He can imagine her with bright red lipstick, smothering foundation, too-much blush. "Yes, sir," she finally admits with swollen pride. "And I wouldn't have it any other way."

"What about a husband?" Reality swelled back into place. Lorelei shakes her head yet shows no emotion on her aged face. Peter rolls his gaze around the bedroom and into the empty but ornately decorated living space. "No pets?"

She hums for a moment, as if gathering the courage to speak. Her posture begins to fail her as the words drop out. "I had one."

Lorelei Coffin : *Part Two*

Colorful and pungent chips trickled into a clean, ceramic bowl. Muted tittering against the slick surface further stifled once it was full. Lorelei felt a pull in her back as she rested the bowl onto a raised wooden platform. Wispy mewing sourced from her calico cat. Each one was unusually breathy for a healthy feline.

Light steps from her leathery paws tracked from the carpet and into the kitchen. The woman watched her pet approach the bowl out of obligation rather than genuine hunger. "You're sick, Vicky-kitty?" No sound of confirmation. The greying cat sniffed the contents and instead decided to lap from the adjacent bowl of water. "Yeah. You're not feeling too well." This was said in a strident lisp, as were most of her conversations with the cat.

"Try not to puke on anything," Lorelei nervously sang while gathering a handful of items. A blanched designer handbag pilfered from an estate sale, an umbrella, and a gaudy turquoise necklace given to her by her niece. In a stiff voice, just as she was exiting her home: "If you do, clean it up before I get home."

She hung in the doorway for a moment, expecting an answer from the lethargic critter. With a prayer under her breath, Lorelei locked the door behind her—careful to twist the knob thrice and push in with her shoulder once out of aggressively habitual caution.

The elevator taken for her short descent was rather spacious. Many individuals in her apartment complex, she had noticed, were disabled in some way. The detail regarding accessibility was indeed the reason why she renewed her lease time and again. Even walking to her car was beginning to wind her. Soon, she thought, I'll be in a wheelchair just like Vinny's daughter.

Or with a walker, just how my mother was.

-

Lorelei's preferred salon was a tiny establishment not too far from the cemetery her dear mother rested at. She consciously drove a route that prevented her from passing by the many headstones. The thought of visiting always stuck with her during those trips—imagining the peace she would find being so close to death yet triumphing as a victor. The woman did not know where her old friends and enemies were within the site, or whether their families decided on elaborate tombs rather than wimpy, easily missed markers.

She had decided long ago on cremation for herself. If the ashes were shelved in some cool, dark room, never to be claimed or dusted, then so be it. There were so few people to call, no next-of-kin. Her sister was living the life in Bali as a meditation coach for disillusioned, white tourists.

Lost souls who hope to do the minimum yet still want to receive a message from the voice of God himself, she mulled with flared nostrils.

Her chin lifted while adjusting the sun visor. With her air conditioning gone, the ten minute stretch of highway was the most miserable part of her journey. She was afraid to pray for clouds for the possibility of the Lord ignoring her request always seemed high. Lorelei convinced herself that He would have better things to do.

Traffic in Rockville was usually light on Sunday mornings given that many families were already in church or taking strolls along any of the several community parks her town boasted. As much as her faith remained true, the idea of visiting a claustrophobic building and singing ancient hymns with a dead-eyed communion never appealed to her. Her relationship with God was a personal one, where they were ostensibly both comfortable with maintaining a once-a-week phone call via cupped hands and bruised knees.

"'Trust and obey'," her lips parted enough to enunciate the latter-half of her words. One of the old hymns her mother would sing while doing dishes. "'For there's no other way to be happy in Jesus but to trust…'" Lorelei interrupted herself by yawning. Instinctively, her foot eased on the brake while her eyes squeezed tight.

The woman's vehicle was merging into a lane that would lead her through a neighborhood. Through the teary slits that were her eyes, she witnessed a truck in front of her swerve with a sudden jerk to the right. Adrenaline ran through her body for the first time in what felt like years. Her eyesight cleared and she locked her shoulders while gripping the wheel in dedication to keep her car on a straight path.

One glance to her rearview mirror renewed her idea of safety. She resumed breathing and felt a strain on her lungs. Just a moment later, she understood what warranted the truck driver's actions.

A smeared corpse of a cat decorated the side of the road, just feet from an empty lot with a row of trees that could have been her home. Tiny eyes belonging to kittens glinted in the sun as if diamond-like tears were glued to their eyelids. They marched around the corpse in a haphazard dance.

By the time Lorelei was parked in front of NuStyle, her face was damp with tears. What little makeup she decided to put on for the day was compromised.

-

A hard seat welcomed her bulky behind. The egregious curve of the salon chair further upset her knotted spine. She was fine with ignoring the discomfort while ten fingers massaged her skull under hot water. This specific but brief moment of bliss solidified her name as a permanent fixture on the shop's calendar.

"You don't do it this long with your other clients," Lorelei flirted with her stylist. The man laughed but his triangular jaw did not budge.

"I could have stopped a minute ago," Vasiliy commented. He was fixated with the sulfate-laden foam that expanded under her loose curls. From this angle, the man focused on where the coy layer of foundation was not properly blended. "But, I know how much you love it."

"Mm-hm."

Lorelei inhaled the vibrant scents until they became a part of her. In another life, she, too, would have been a beautician if her sister had not beaten her to it first. "I never wanted to be a teacher," she admitted with her eyes sealed shut. "Did I ever tell you that?"

"You have."

"Well, it's true. I know how much I go on about my students. Former students. I don't really think about them that much, but whenever I come here… I can't help but slip into old memories."

Vasiliy expressed his understanding with a slow groan. He began rinsing her hair free from the product. "I'm your therapist, eh?"

She scoffed and opened one eye. "About as expensive as one."

"Maybe I should ask you why you were crying, then?" The woman froze. He could feel the tension emanate from her body. "No obligation, Lorelei. You know, I'm not *actually* your therapist."

"No, no. It's okay. You've got a good eye." His smile beamed with intelligence, as if the smudged makeup and reddened eyes were not any sort of indication. The woman drew in a shallow breath through her nose and exhaled via a loose raspberry. "I saw something horrible, Vasiliy. Just—just so horrible on my way here."

The stylist kept quiet while working with her delicate hair. He noticed streaks of silver were blanching her already platinum blonde hair. "Sorry, but I have to ask. Are you finally interested in a dye-job?"

"Oh, sweet Lord. No." He lifted his hands in defeat. "You ask me this every damn time. What was I saying?"

With closed intonation, the man defended his case. "Lorelei, your natural hair color is so beautiful and I can recreate it in just a few hours. At least think about it, eh?"

She reset her shoulders and pouted. The pressure of his words bore down on her body like a hot, weighted blanket. "A few hours. I have to get home soon."

"Ri-i-ight. A hot date?" Vasiliy turned to dry his hands on a towel hanging from a counter full of his equipment.

The woman scoffed. "Maybe hot diarrhea." Lorelei's eyes cracked open and witnessed an expression of disgust from a stylist adjacent to her chair.

She held in a chuckle as Vasiliy apologized on her behalf. "Goodness, woman. What on earth?" He hid the blush from his cheeks by masking his face with either hand. Through a harsh yet playful whisper: "You're going to get me fired."

Lorelei rolled her eyes. She felt naked as those in the salon passed lukewarm glances her way. "Oh, everybody needs to calm their horses. My cat is sick, that's all. Poor baby's been off since around yesterday morning."

Casually, "Ah, yeah. Yours too?" He revealed a plastic tail comb and instructed her to relax by tapping her shoulders. Refusing the request, she craned her neck to him.

"Who else has a sick cat?"

"Like, two other of my clients. Another one's cat just died, actually." Vasiliy's tone became somber as if a genuine depression set upon him. "Cutest thing. Only three, too. Yo!" He lifted his chin and called another stylist. "Gary!"

An older gentleman with silver hair and small, round glasses perched upon the bridge of his nose reluctantly answered. His voice was tired. "Yes, Vas?" Pulling away from his client seemed to be the greatest offense fathomable.

"You have a cat, eh?" Lorelei and her stylist watched the man nod with complete disinterest. "It's doing okay, yeah?"

"Just fine," Gary said through a sigh. "Thanks for asking."

The old woman could not shake the anxiety that swung through her limbs and between her ribs. Syllables formed on the middle of her tongue and halted before the tip. Her thin lips twisted without a sound.

Vasiliy scratched his neck with the back of his right wrist. "You okay, dear?"

"I'd rather… If it's okay, I… Well, I guess I have to finish…"

An audible inhale through his nostrils. He stepped in front of her and crouched at eye-level. She searched his face and found compassion. "Your baby is going to be okay."

Weakly, "I just want to go home." The man nodded with a dull smile that was a distant companion to his sentiment.

-

Lorelei's monthly self-care day had been ruined. It was the one thing she allowed herself to indulge in. Fifty-five dollars and I can't even enjoy it, she seethed. Her short but labored march up one flight of stairs added to the stress she held on to.

The elevator she so relied on was once again out of service. Any time a storm brewed nearby, a sure bet was that the electronics in her mid-century apartment complex would go haywire.

At least there will be rain, the woman sighed.

There was a strain on her joints that she has not had to endure for months. An angry hand made of lava gripped her spine, each segment melted and seeped into her nerves. A persistent splintering under the balls of her knees exhausted her just by thinking of how to mend them. She imagined an epsom salt bath would help, maybe a new kind of cream that was suggested to her the last time she visited Foodsmart.

When Lorelei finally reached the apex of the stairs, she took a deep breath and thought of how to navigate cleaning up any sick her cat might have left. The lingering and aggressive pain in her body prevented the simple movement of turning the key into its lock. Before anything, she thought, I need water.

The door popped open and she pushed her way into the apartment. There was indeed a scent, like saccharine phlegm or sour dairy. Her heart fell from her chest to her feet. "Vicky-kitty?" She sang.

A weak response from the cat that was hidden somewhere in the apartment. An unusual staccato of a mew. Lorelei tried again while moving through the house, keeping her eyes to the already matted and filthy carpet she never had the energy to steam.

Each step sent a shock of pain up her spine. Half of the cleaning supplies were under the sink and the other half rested at the bottom of a shelf where her linens and spare blankets were kept. The closer she got to the kitchen, the stronger the unusual scent became and the more she wanted to lay down and worry about it later.

In the center of the tile, laying between the fridge and a counter, was her shuddering cat. Vicky did not look at her while foam billowed from its mouth. She kept cool by keeping her stomach against the unswept tiled floor.

The first thing Lorelei noticed was her cat's coarse, patchy fur. "Oh, baby girl." Her nostrils expanded and fought back a swell of tears. She crouched to the ground and a crack from her achy knees startled the despondent critter.

Vicky jumped and scanned the kitchen. Seeing her owner did not help to calm her nerves. "Kitty-kitty-baby?" The animal hummed a dry tone, her head bobbing as if trying her hardest to stay awake. "Sweety-pie?"

The woman felt two hot tears roll, one after another. She began to sing a song to her beloved pet, the only one that has been on her mind. "Trust and obey, f-for there's n-no other way…" Lorelei heaved one wet sob and Vicky turned to face her. A lackluster veil draped over the cat's eyes.

Deep panting, as if all moisture had been drained from the creature's body. She stared, immobile and in obvious pain. Lorelei would later understand that she felt the same way. Crouching low to the ground did not help her joints.

Feeling a strained pressure in her spine, the woman reached out to grab the counter with her left hand while anchoring back to her feet. She kept her groans of frustration to herself. Though she fought off tears, her eyes never moved away from the animal.

-

Peter's cell phone screen lights up and flashes the time. Almost eleven at night. He sucks in a yawn. Lorelei's voice croaks, "What, you want something to eat?"

"I don't mean to interrupt. Could I, though?"

"You have to go make it, though. I don't have the energy to mess around with pots and pans."

He shakes his head. "Something light should be fine. A snack, really. Graham crackers, or…" Her laugh catches him off-guard, and in-turn, he cracks a smile. "What?"

"Of all the things. I have animal crackers if you're so inclined." The woman's tone was playful. The energy surrounding her attitude suits her, Peter internally settles.

She tells him where in the kitchen and in which shelf they should be. When he enters the tile, his feet freeze in place. Even from the other room, the woman notices this. "The—the one above the sink. Hello?" His return is silent. In his right hand

is a worn box, a generic brand of animal crackers with shapes he

can scarcely recognize. "Get lost?"

"No, I… Honestly," his eyes stick to the graphic on the

box. A cartoon parade of typical zoo animals. "Your story. It's

the same kitchen you saw Vicky, right?"

Lorelei swallows and expresses an airy groan. Peter

apologizes, but she shoos the sentiment away. "It's been long

enough. Yes. Same kitchen."

He wishes to dive into the box and stuff his mouth with

the more-than-likely stale junk food, but knows that he risks

offending her by still having an appetite. The man settles on one,

very soft animal cracker for now.

After chewing, Peter asks, "Can I be blunt with you?"

She blinks once, then cocks her shoulder in a half-hearted shrug.

Some exhaustion is now clear on her face. Heavier eye-lids, a relaxed jaw. "Well, not so much me being blunt as just asking if you… If you had to kill her?"

Immediately, "I don't like that." She rubs the well of her throat. Lucidity returns to her. "I really don't want to talk about that." If Lorelei weren't so exhausted, she would boot him out herself—toss him into the hallway by the elastic of his pants and pat her hands dry before slamming the door on his face.

"I'm sorry. Just—hey, just know that I've been through it, too." His tone is suspicious, even to him.

"You had to kill your cat?"

Peter's left eye twitches as he loads his response. "Well…" She leans forward.

"You had—had to wrap it up in a towel? Use a hammer, too? Hm! Or what, did you have a *gun*?" The man lowers the box to his lap and begins wrapping up the crackers without a word. "If you tell me that you faced down your own cat and—and…"

Lorelei's head bobs side-to-side. Her eyes wag in a frantic examination of his face. Both of her nostrils wildly flare without much rhythm.

Peter tosses the box aside and moves in front of the woman, resting on his right knee and holding either of her hips. "Lorelei? Hey, hey. I'm going to call the ambulance."

Even through all of the obvious pain, the strenuous effort to keep herself from wailing, she manages to send out a final call of rebellion: "N-no. D-don't. Too much."

"I'll pay for it. I have a good job. I have a really good job."

With every blink, her eyelashes stick for longer and longer. Peter calms his own breathing and counts each breath, subtly instructing her to do the same. As soon as his phone is removed from the suffocatingly deep pocket of his oversized slacks, he begins dialing.

She can not hear the conversation. A consistent ebb and flow of an aggressive ocean washes over the canals in her ears. A tribal beat plays upon either eardrum, though it is louder in her right ear. Heat fills the same side of her face.

Lorelei manages to contract her fingers and feels a dull pressure of where her nails meet her palms. There is not enough sensation. Peter pulls her attention towards him by moving his face in her line of sight. His mouth moves—she can see this through the blinds that are her damp eyelashes. She watches the shape of his uneven lips twist and contort until the image of his face becomes still.

He does not move, and she is not able to. A static hum accompanies a sinking feeling that resonates in the center of her forehead. The image of the gaunt man constricts into a fine point in the center of her vision; an icy hand reaches through the ether to clutch every bit of her reality and steals it away with an abrupt inhale.

Joey & Sarah is written to be a love letter to identifying the inner-child and healing them. Quite a few new issues can arise when others are looked at.

Wyatt & Gene is written through a satirical lens that most individuals share. The idea of "what if"—the absurd scenarios that tend to form in one's head when under stress or directly after a particularly loathsome interaction.

Cade & Tawny is about a love so real and intrinsic that it begets death even while evading it.

Francine & Corey is an homage to the windfall of conspiracies that distort our reality. Not all distortions are negative.

Lorelei Coffin represents the unknown; how easily structure can both thrive and disappear within the same day.

About The Author

Cody George is obsessed with petting dogs and writing about them.

In this anthology series, his focus shifts to the opposite side of the spectrum with *cats*—the archetype of which encompasses each interrelated story.

Isolation, distrusting, cold.

How can warmth return to a world that forsakes intimacy? By allowing oneself to be immersed in healing through the method of egoless communication. The characters in *A Reconciliation With Death* each struggle with being alone. Without parents, without a partner, without a friend, without a pet—one can stabilize a connection with self through intimacy with others.

First written in October, 2019. Well before the COVID-19 pandemic.

keep up to date with the author:

twitter: @ggghhhost

follow the cover artist

twitter: @d0gtier

special thanks to *shea callanan* for proofreading

ISBN-13: 978-0578727912

Whistling Pirates

Whistling Pines book 5

Dean L. Hovey

Print ISBNs
Amazon Print 978 0 2286 1732 7
LSI Print 978 0 2286 1733 4
B&N Print 978 0 2286 1734 1

BWL Publishing Inc.

Books we love to write ...
Authors around the world.

http://bwlpublishing.ca

9 780578 727912